Trish Wylie worked on a long career of careers to get to the one she wanted from her late teens. She flicked her blonde hair over her shoulder while playing the promotions game, patted her manicured hands on the backs of musicians in the music business, smiled sweetly at awkward customers during the retail nightmare known as the run-up to Christmas, and has got completely lost in her car in every single town in Ireland while working as a sales rep. And it took all that character-building and a healthy sense of humour to get her dream job, she feels—where she spends her days in reindeer slippers, with her hair in whatever band she can find to keep it out of the way, make-up as vague and distant a memory as manicured nails, while she gets to create the kind of dream man she'd still like to believe is out there somewhere. If it turns out he is, she promises she'll let you know...after she's been out for a new wardrobe, a manicure and a make-over...

Praise for
Trish Wylie:

'Another fantastic novel by Trish Wylie
which you will devour in a single sitting!
Brimming with passion, emotion, romance
and humour, and featuring a fantastic heroine
and a gorgeous hero...sheer perfection!'
—*CataRomance* on O'REILLY'S BRIDE

'With its splendid cast of amiable characters,
hilarious one-liners, heartwarming romance
and powerful emotional intensity...another triumph
for the hugely talented Trish Wylie, one of the
brightest stars of contemporary romance!'
—*CataRomance* on PROJECT: PARENTHOOD

'Absolutely wonderful! Trish Wylie's spellbinding
tale will tickle your funny bone and tug at your
heartstrings. Featuring characters which leap off the
pages, realistic dialogue, sweet romance, sizzling
sex scenes, electrifying sexual tension and dramatic
emotional intensity...feel-good romance at its finest!'
—*CataRomance* on WHITE-HOT

THE INCONVENIENT LAWS OF ATTRACTION

BY
TRISH WYLIE

All the characters in this book have no existence outside the imagination of the author, and have no relation whatsoever to anyone bearing the same name or names. They are not even distantly inspired by any individual known or unknown to the author, and all the incidents are pure invention.

First published in Great Britain 2011
by Mills & Boon, an imprint of Harlequin (UK) Limited.
Harlequin (UK) Limited, Eton House, 18-24 Paradise Road,
Richmond, Surrey TW9 1SR

ISBN: 978 0 263 22142 8

Harlequin (UK) policy is to use papers that are natural, renewable and recyclable products and made from wood grown in sustainable forests. The logging and manufacturing process conform to the legal environmental regulations of the country of origin.

Printed and bound in Great Britain
by CPI Antony Rowe, Chippenham, Wiltshire

Also by Trish Wylie:

BREATHLESS!
BRIDE OF THE EMERALD ISLE
CLAIMED BY THE BILLIONAIRE BAD BOY
HER ONE AND ONLY VALENTINE
HER REAL-LIFE HERO
HER UNEXPECTED BABY

For everyone who kept me from hitting the ground
until I remembered how to fly again.

CHAPTER ONE

'OLIVIA BRANNIGAN. Blake Clayton?'

Continuing to rehearse below her breath, she tugged firmly on her jacket as she walked up the path. 'I represent Wagner, Liebstrahm, Barker and DeLuise, and…'

It was what came after the 'and' she was struggling with most. Informing him of a legacy was one thing, breaking the news that came with it was another, even if the news was several weeks old. But the man would have to live in a cave to have avoided hearing about it and they couldn't have been *that* close—not when it had taken so long to find him.

The Stars And Stripes hanging from the porch fluttered gently in a welcome hint of air movement as she took a deep breath and pressed the buzzer.

'I regret to have to inform you…'

She hated that line. Last time she'd made a death notification it had been more than difficult: It had been the final act in a series of events that altered the course of her life.

When the door swung open, a heavy-set man holding a half-eaten hamburger looked her over from head to toe.

'Mr Clayton?'

'Yo, Blake!' he yelled.

'What?' a voice yelled in answer.

'Anyone suing you?'

'Not this week.'

'Guess you can come in then.' The man grinned, issuing an invitation with a jerk of his head.

Following him down the hallway, Olivia's heels clicked in an even, businesslike rhythm while she focused on their destination and the man she would discover when she got there. In a matter of seconds he would be a living, breathing person instead of someone she'd spent entirely too much time trying to picture in her mind while she was searching for him. She wouldn't have to imagine what he looked like or wonder how he was going to react.

The mystery would be solved.

Anticipation built with each step as she prepared for the disappointment of reality when compared to the uncharacteristic flights of fantasy she'd been engaged in of late. There was just something about this case that got to her, and with her track record when it came to emotional involvement in the workplace, that wasn't good.

The sooner she wrapped it up, the better.

The room she walked into was in a chaotic state of construction. There were four men in it: two chewing hamburgers, one hunkered down sanding a door-frame and another by large windows covered in opaque plastic. Since the man by the windows was looking at her, she approached him and held out a hand. 'Mr Clayton, I'm Olivia Brannigan from—'

'Over here, sweetheart.' A deep, rough-edged voice drew her gaze to the man sanding the door-frame.

'You're Blake Clayton?' She turned around. Considering how long it had taken to find him, she had to be sure. 'Blake *Anders* Clayton.'

There was a snort of laughter behind her.

'Thanks for that.' He shook his head, dropping his chin

and lifting a hand to remove the dust mask from his face as he stood up. 'So what'd I do this time?'

Opening her mouth to set his mind at ease, anything resembling coherent thought scrambled when he set the mask aside and looked directly at her. The room contracted; it was suddenly smaller and tighter and felt as if all the oxygen had been sucked out of it. Everything in her peripheral vision blurred as her gaze locked on him and doggedly refused to let go. But who could blame a girl for staring?

A little heads-up on how he looked might have helped.

Six foot two, possibly three, lean at the waist, broad at the shoulders, with short spikes of unruly chocolate-brown hair and dark eyes that sparkled with more than a hint of the guy a girl's mother would warn her about; Blake Clayton was the living, breathing definition of *seriously smokin' hot*.

When her gaze dropped briefly to the jut of a full lower lip that begged for immediate, audience-be-damned attention, Olivia ran her tongue over her teeth. Would he taste as good as he looked? She'd just bet he did.

The woman inside her purred appreciatively. The professional forced a businesslike tone to her voice. 'I represent the legal firm of Wagner, Liebstrahm, Barker and DeLuise, and—'

'Bet that's a bitch to put on a business card.' A corner of his mouth hitched with amusement.

The woman sighed contentedly while the professional frowned at how difficult it was to focus. Her flights of fantasy had fallen woefully short of reality.

'Is there somewhere we could talk?'

'We're talking now.'

'Mr Clayton, I'm afraid I have bad news,' she announced more bluntly than she'd intended.

'I heard,' he said tightly, the change in him immediate.

Her voice softened 'I'm sorry for your loss.'

'Don't be.' Stepping past her to lift a mug from a worktop, he sat down beside one of the men eating lunch, spreading long, jeans-clad legs while tipping the rim of the mug to his mouth. 'We done?'

Glancing at their audience, she found them watching her like some kind of floor show. Surely he didn't want to—

'You can say whatever you have to say in front of them,' he added as if he'd read her mind.

Considering her thoughts since she'd laid eyes on him, Olivia sincerely hoped he hadn't.

'No secrets among friends,' the man who'd answered the door added. 'Offer us the right money, we could tell you enough to get him arrested in a half-dozen states.'

'And Canada,' added a chorus of voices.

'You got something you need me to sign, hand it over,' Blake said over the sound of laughter. 'You can mail whatever memento I've got coming my way.'

'I'm afraid I can't do that,' Olivia replied patiently. 'You're the sole beneficiary. He left everything to you.'

'Everything?'

'Yes.'

'All of it?'

'Yes.' She nodded. He obviously hadn't known. Not that the flat tone to his deep voice gave any indication he was happy with the news. The majority of people would have been turning cartwheels.

'There's no one else?'

Confused by the question after her use of the term 'sole beneficiary', she shook her head. 'No.' Thanks to Charles Warren's will, his son was one of the richest, most powerful men in America. 'I know it must seem daunting to take on the responsibility of—'

'Such a great legacy?' A dark brow lifted. 'Wrong tactic, Miss—what did you say your name was again?'

'Brannigan.' She tried not to be piqued by the fact he hadn't remembered. 'Olivia Brannigan.'

'Well, *Liv*—' he leaned forward '—someone should probably have warned you: I don't give a rat's ass how great a legacy it is. I don't want it.'

Was he *insane*?

'I understand you need time to process everything, b—'

'There's nothing to process.' Setting his mug down, he pushed to his feet. 'What I *need* is to get this job done.'

As she faltered, he walked past her and picked up his tools. She'd never been in such a surreal situation. What did he expect her to do? Go back to the office, walk up to her boss and say, *Sorry, no go, we have to find someone else we can give billions of dollars' worth of property and assets to?* They could hold a raffle.

When she didn't move, he glanced at her from the corner of his eye. 'Am I supposed to tip you?'

Seriously?

The professional stepped forward and smiled smoothly. 'I don't think you understand, Mr Clayton. Allow me to make it clear: you're it. Whether you want it or not, you're the sole beneficiary of Charles Warren's will.'

'*The* Charles Warren?' an incredulous voice asked behind her.

'Your father made his wishes very clear.'

'Father?' said the same incredulous voice. 'You're kidding me, right?'

So much for no secrets between friends…

He took a step forward and lowered his voice. 'Look, lady, I get that you're trying to do your job but, in case you didn't get it, allow *me* to make it clear: *I'm not your man.* So unless you're planning on setting down that briefcase and picking up a power tool, I suggest you hightail it back to Manhattan and tell Wagner, Liebstrahm, Barker and DeLuise—or whoever it is you answer to further down the food chain—they best find a distant Warren relative they can lay this on. I have a life. I'm not living someone else's.'

'This isn't going anywhere,' she insisted with a deceptive calmness that masked the effect his proximity was having on her body.

'Maybe not,' he allowed. 'But *I* can.'

What about the life he'd said he had? Olivia found herself wondering if there was a woman in it; one who would miss him when he was gone. Somehow she doubted he was the type to stick around long enough to let anyone get that close. Judging by the number of addresses she'd discovered in various different states—some of which he'd only resided in for a matter of weeks—any relationships he had were short-lived. Not that looking the way he did would leave him short of company for long.

Squaring her shoulders, she reached into the front of the briefcase he'd mentioned and held out her hand. 'I'll leave my card. When you've had time to think things over—'

'Not gonna happen.'

Olivia stood her ground.

'I take it you can find the door on your own?'

Okay. If he wanted to play hardball, she'd play. Lowering her gaze to his broad chest, she relaxed her shoulders and took a step forward, standing within inches of his large body and slowly lifting her lashes until she was looking deep into dark eyes. She ran her tongue over her lips and smoothed them together, watching his gaze lower and smiling when he frowned. She spoke in a low voice just loud enough for their audience to hear.

'Tomorrow morning...all over the state...thousands of

Warren Enterprises employees are going to turn up for work. I'd like to be able to tell them they'll have a job a month from now, especially in this economy.' She angled her head. 'Wouldn't you?'

Reaching out, she set her business card on a plank of wood beside him before turning on her heel and walking back down the hall. Her hand was on the door when she heard a voice ask, 'Charles Warren is your old man?'

Silence.

'You know my cousin Mike works for Warren Tech? He's got a wife and three kids…'

Olivia smiled as she opened the door. There was no question in her mind she'd be seeing him again.

She was looking forward to it already.

Blake had always liked cities better than small towns. Cities were anonymous, no one wanted to poke their nose in anyone else's business; it was easy to disappear into the crowd in the city. At least it used to be…

'Isn't that your lawyer lady from the other day?'

'Yup.' He'd known she was there from the minute she appeared with her mismatched set of friends. His gaze found her in the crowded bar with the same accuracy as a heat-seeking missile.

'Sure fills out a pair of jeans,' Marty observed.

'I'm sure Chrissy will be glad to hear you noticed.'

'I'm married, not blind.'

Without her power suit she was different, there was no denying that. Dressed in hip-hugging jeans and a scoop-necked blouse that highlighted her narrow waist, pale skin and the swell of her breasts, it had been hard to ignore her presence since she arrived. If there'd been the remotest chance they might cross paths again, he would never have accepted Marty's usual end-of-the-working-week invitation for a beer and a game of pool in the nearest bar to the restoration project they'd been working on in the West Village. But it was too late now. It was only a matter of time before she crossed the room.

Bending over to line up his shot, Blake's gaze was drawn upward by the appearance of distinctly feminine, jeans-clad thighs at the other side of the table.

'Gentlemen…'

And there she was.

Sinking a ball into the pocket in front of her before standing upright, he set the end of his cue on the floor, folding his fingers around it as he looked her over.

American pool halls had once been the exclusive realm of men who smoked cigars and drank beer while they growled and spit tobacco. Young truants cleaned tables and floors, racking balls for new games while they learnt pool hustling and miscreant behaviour. It had been a poor man's men's club, devoid of female company.

Blake couldn't help thinking it would have been better for Olivia Brannigan if it had stayed that way.

Because the second his gaze swept over her, he had the exact same reaction he'd had the first time. The tips of his fingers itched to be thrust into her sleek blond mane and mess it up until it framed her face the way it would after a session of the kind of hot, sweaty, mutually gratifying sex he doubted she'd ever experienced. He wanted to set the pad of his thumb on her full lips and smear away any hint of lipstick before he set his mouth on hers, to place a palm to the small of her back, melding her body to his as—

He took a measured breath. 'Want to play, do you?'

'So it would seem.'

There was a brief spark of light in the cool blue of her eyes that suggested a challenge did it for her. The fact she'd answered in a low voice which could easily have been described as sultry didn't escape him either.

'Reckon you can take me on?'

'I guess we'll find out, won't we?'

Indeed they would.

'Rack 'em up, Marty.'

While Marty handed over his cue and started gathering balls from the pockets, Blake stepped around the table to issue a low warning. 'If you're over here to discuss my luck in the legacy department, you can forget it.'

'Well, I don't know about you,' she replied brightly, 'but *I'm* off the clock.'

Looking down at her from the corner of his eye, he saw her check the face of a neat wristwatch. A wave of softly curled hair hid her profile from him until she lifted her chin and added, 'As of an hour and ten minutes ago.'

'You're the kind of gal who's never off the clock.'

'Maybe you don't know me as well as you like to think you do.'

'Meaning I should get to know you better?'

'We're set,' Marty said.

Blake held out an arm. 'Ladies first.'

'Don't hold back on my account.'

He leaned towards her as he walked by. 'Never do.'

'She know what she's doing?' Marty asked as he joined him at the bar.

Time would tell. Since every town had a pool table, they'd been one of the few constants in Blake's life growing up. He knew a lot of pool was simple physics. Watching men who'd been playing for most of their lives, he knew it was all about the angles, the action and reaction, knowing when to exert a little force and when to use a finer touch. He'd learnt a lot of valuable life lessons from the game of pool. Watching Olivia Brannigan in action turned it into something altogether different: less physics, a whole lot more to do with chemistry.

Didn't matter which side of the table she took her shot from, either way it provided the kind of view any red-blooded male could appreciate. When she was on the far side of the table, bending over the cue, it allowed a clean line of sight down her blouse to a hint of coloured ribbon that became the equivalent of an apple in Eden. A side view let his gaze skim over the sweep of her spine, the sweet curve of her ass, down legs that would never have ended if it hadn't been for the floor.

As a card-carrying one hundred per cent red-blooded male, his body's reaction to her was understandable. *Unwelcome*, considering what she represented, but understandable. Not to mention a timely reminder he'd obviously been all work and no play for too long. Something he would have to rectify, soon.

Standing upright, her gaze collided with his as she walked around the table with a hint of a smile on her face. Turning, she bent over to line up her next shot, gently swaying her hips from side to side: *right in front of him.*

'She's good,' Marty said appreciatively as a ball ricocheted off a cushion directly into a corner pocket.

Blake's silent agreement had nothing to do with her pool skills. Setting his bottle down, he stepped towards her. 'Hustling me, Liv?'

'It's Olivia,' she informed him, twisting on her heel and backing away with a sweet smile. 'And if I wanted to hustle you, wouldn't it make more sense to play badly before making a wager?'

'You just popped over here to play a friendly little game of pool with the boys?'

Standing still long enough to efficiently chalk the tip of

her cue with short, sharp movements, she continued walking around the table. 'Is that illegal?'

'You're the lawyer. You tell me.'

'I know it's not in the state of New York.' She bent down. 'But I'd have to check the rules for Canada.'

When another ball disappeared off the table, she smiled a small, satisfied smile as she stood up.

'I'm not talking to you about the will.'

'I didn't ask you to.'

'You're going to.'

'You can see into the future?' A flicker of amusement sparkled in her eyes. 'Wouldn't happen to know next week's lottery numbers, would you?' She shrugged a shoulder as she walked around the table.

'Not that you need them.'

'You know I can take out a restraining order against everyone at your firm if I have to…'

'Be a pretty long list of names.'

'I'd know who to put at the top.'

When he set his palm on the wooden edge of the table as she bent over her cue again, a brief upward flicker of her lashes revealed what might almost have been taken for hesitation. Did she realise she was playing in the big leagues? *Good.* Considering her options? *More likely.* Looking back down the cue, she swayed her hips again, a move that could have been misconstrued as preparation for her next shot to the untrained eye. Blake recognised it for what it was.

What bugged him was how well it was working.

'I didn't know you'd be here, if that's what you're suggesting,' she said in a matter-of-fact tone.

That he was more likely to believe. How could she when he hadn't known himself until a little under an hour ago? He never did from one Friday to the next. It was the nature of the job, the story of his life.

There was a sharp click and another ball disappeared off the table. 'But, since we are here, maybe if you told me what the problem is, we could talk about it.'

'We could—' he rocked forward as she stood up '—if I hadn't already said I *wasn't* talking about it.'

'You brought it up.'

'Pity you're off the clock then, isn't it?'

She sighed. 'It's a lot of money to ignore.'

If money meant as much to him as she seemed to think it should, she might have a point. Rocking back on his heels, Blake stilled, his gaze scanning the crowd. He wondered what she'd think if she knew, given the option, he'd prefer every cent to disappear. He didn't want to be responsible for thousands of people's lives. A rolling stone could end up looking like the Rockies if it gathered that much moss.

'I know it's an intimidating prospect, running a company that large—' her voice softened to a hum that washed across his senses with the same burn as the first sip of a smooth Scotch '—but there are people who have been with the company for decades…'

She was playing the guilt card again? When he looked down at her from the corner of his eye, she tacked on a soft smile and added, 'They could run it for you.'

'That's exactly what I—'

Blake set an arm across Marty's chest when he stepped forward to add his two cents.

'You think I'm avoiding this because the leap from carpenter to CEO is beyond me?'

'I didn't say that.'

Not in so many words. But she was smarter than that.

Tucking the cue into the crook of his arm, he folded his arms across his chest. 'So you're gonna do what? Talk me through a pie chart? Help me pick out a suit for the office? Hold my hand while I go play with the big boys?' He narrowed his eyes and smiled tightly. 'Don't think I don't know what you're doing, sweetheart.'

'It's called trying to help.'

'That's going well.' He nodded. 'For future reference—insulting my intelligence? Not a good place to start.'

Stepping around her to get to the bar, he lifted his bottle and tilted it to his mouth. His gaze followed her in the mirror as she followed him.

'I wasn't trying to insult you,' she said in the sultry tone that travelled directly from ear to groin.

Blake gritted his teeth. Sure she wasn't.

'Would hardly be the best way to start a working relationship, would it?'

What working relationship?

'It's really none of my business why you want to turn your back on billions of dollars. But, like I said, the responsibility isn't going anywhere. The board's hands are tied. You have controlling interest in the company—they can't do anything without your say-so. It's how your father wanted it.'

The woman didn't know when to quit.

Her voice lowered. 'I know you're still grieving. The last thing you want right now is—'

'Grieving?' A burst of sarcastic laughter split the air as he set his bottle down with a slam and turned on her, frustration mixing with anger. 'Lady, you don't know anything about—'

'Blake...' Marty used a hand on his upper arm to hold him still and allow him time to take a breath; his voice was filled with the same rock-steady calmness he'd used in the old days when Blake had been prone to standing up to guys twice his size. It had been the curse of the new kid and since Blake had always been the new kid...

With a nod from Blake to indicate he was good, Marty

stepped away. Blake looked at Olivia and saw she was staring at him with a mixture of suspicion and curiosity. Not fear, he noted. Part of him respected the hell out of her for that when guys much bigger than her had been known to baulk. It was enough to make him step towards her again; the fact she stood her ground increased his perception of her as a woman who could hold her own.

He shook his head when his libido buzzed with the numerous possibilities that came with the thought. Strong women who could take him on both in and out of the bedroom—preferably without needing emotional entanglement—did it for him. Always had, always would.

He took a short breath. 'As much of a pain in the ass as you're proving to be, you didn't deserve that.'

She arched a brow. 'Is that an apology?'

'It's as close as I ever get to giving one.' A corner of his mouth tugged wryly. 'I'd run with it if I were you.'

Considering him with a tilt of her head, she came back with, 'Know what you could do to make it up to me?'

Wasn't going to like this, was he?

'You know what the Warren Foundation is?'

And now he was an idiot again.

'They're hosting a benefit a couple of weeks from now. If you showed up—even for an hour or two—you might encourage people to reach deeper into their pockets to impress the new owner of the company.' She shrugged as if she didn't care one way or another if he showed. 'As well as helping a worthy cause, you can meet some of the people who work for you in a social environment.'

'You're one of those women who calls in the middle of the night to tell a guy his phone is ringing, aren't you?'

When she continued calmly holding his gaze, Blake wondered if she ever cut loose. What would it take to get the real Olivia Brannigan to come on down and—the question immediately jumped to the front of his mind—just how far was she willing to go to get what she wanted?

He was tempted to find out.

'It's at the Empire hotel,' she added with a nod as if he'd already agreed, her gaze lowering to travel over his body from the middle of his chest to the toes of his boots.

Digging in the pocket of his jeans as he turned away, Blake frowned at the immediate response the invisible touch had on him. 'I'll think about it.'

'It's formal. You'll need a tux.'

'I said I'll think about it.' Tossing several bills on the bar, he turned to face her again. 'While I do, I suggest you think about what you're getting yourself into.'

'Meaning?'

He stepped closer, forcing her to lift her chin. Searching her eyes, he noted the spark it took a blink of long lashes to conceal and smiled a slow smile. As aware of him as he was of her, wasn't she? Unless he was mistaken—which he doubted—she'd known exactly what she was doing around the pool table. She thought she was in control of the situation and could use her sexuality to her advantage. He was fine with her attempting the latter, but if she wanted to take him on at more than a simple game of pool there were a few things she needed to understand.

'Meaning you gamble, you best be prepared to ante-up, so think long and hard about what you're bringing to the table, sweetheart.' He closed the gap and moved his face closer to hers, his gaze lowering to her mouth, then shifting sharply to tangle with hers. 'Because I'll collect, and I think you know exactly what I mean by that.'

The almost imperceptible narrowing of her eyes told him she'd got the message. Blake smiled lazily when the next thing he saw was a spark of light that said it was 'game on' as far as she was concerned.

It was enough, for now.

Walking across the crowded room without looking back, he swung open the door and stepped out into oppressively humid air, pacing up and down on the sidewalk while he waited for Marty. Maybe he should just get the hell on with it. The sooner he did something about offloading property, dumping stocks and signing things over to people who might want them, the sooner he could leave it behind and get on with his life. It was more constructive than waiting around for a hint of grief to make an appearance. Especially when the lack of it was starting to make him feel like a heartless son-of-a—

Shouldn't he feel *something*? When he looked inside at the dark corner where he'd tucked away his memories of the past, there was nothing: a big, black vacuum of nothing. That should have made him feel guilty; but nope, still nothing. Not a thing. As if part of him was missing.

When the door swung open again, he made a snap decision. 'Think you can keep an eye on the crew?'

'Sure.' Marty's shrug wouldn't have inspired confidence if Blake hadn't known him better. 'Do what you gotta do, *Anders*.'

That was that, then. Another thought occurred to him and he began to smile as they walked towards the subway station. No reason he couldn't have some fun along the way. Never let it be said he couldn't multitask.

Olivia Brannigan's life was about to get interesting.

CHAPTER TWO

'Now, remember, you can't kill a client.'

Be prepared to ante-up? He would *collect*? Who did he think he was? Inside her head, Olivia was laughing the derogatory laugh of a woman in serious self-denial. But who was she kidding? She hadn't been able to resist a battle of wills since the second grade.

'Potential client,' she corrected, tucking her cellphone between her shoulder and her ear so she could reach into her briefcase. 'And right now I'm not even sure I can work with this guy. He's—'

'Sexy as sin?' Jo asked in a tone that suggested she was batting her eyelashes.

'Not helping.'

Grimacing at the pain from a rapidly growing blister, Olivia checked the address on the folded piece of paper and lifted her gaze to the numbers above the doors in a neat row of brownstones. Being forced across the Brooklyn Bridge in searing midday temperatures to play messenger girl in the most inappropriate heels known to messenger-kind helped—as did the fact he'd demanded the files *immediately.*

Difficult clients she could handle. Raging sexual attraction to a man she might have to work with on a daily basis, *not so much*—and since a simple game of pool had felt a tad too much like foreplay…

Catching sight of a dumpster outside one of the houses, she checked for traffic and crossed the street.

'You know what *would* help?' Jo asked.

'I'm not having sex with him,' she answered firmly, wondering just who it was she was trying to convince. 'He's a *client*.'

'*Potential* client and you can't tell me you haven't thought about it.'

Not under oath she couldn't. Her imagination had been having a field day, particularly in the restless hours she spent tossing and turning in bed before her alarm went off.

The number above the door matched the one on the piece of paper. Olivia's voice lowered to mutter, 'Here we go.'

'I'm just saying…' cajoled the voice in her ear.

'I know. I meant I've got to go. I'm here.'

'Ooh, call me back with the blow-by-blow. I want details. What he's wearing. How he looks. What he says. Don't leave *anything* out!'

Olivia smiled. 'I'm hanging up now.'

With her cellphone tucked safely away in a pocket at the front of her briefcase, she put her jacket on over her sleeveless blouse and buttoned it up as she walked up the steps to the open door, pausing to remove her sunglasses and check her appearance in a nearby window. Loud music echoed from the floor above while she sidestepped debris in the hall and sighed heavily. No air conditioning. *Great.*

'Hello?'

The downstairs rooms were deserted but on the first floor landing the loud squeal of a power tool drew her to a room where she waved a hand to have her presence acknowledged. 'Do you know where I can find Blake Clayton?'

The man pointed upward before continuing his work. On the second floor, she met a semi-naked man in shorts.

'Blake Clayton?'

'Top floor.'

Of course he was. She brushed her shoulder on a wall while trying to avoid a stepladder, and then twisted her neck to search for signs of damage to her jacket as she moved to the next set of stairs. It was getting hotter by the floor. Wasn't hell supposed to be *downstairs*?

'Whoa!' Two large hands grasped her elbows when she caught her heel on a loose floorboard and stumbled forward. 'Careful, lady.'

Scowling briefly at the dusty fingerprints semi-naked man number two had left on her linen sleeves, she forced a smile as she lifted her chin. 'Olivia Brannigan from Wagner, Liebstrahm, Barker and DeLuise. I wonder if—'

'You should get that printed on a T-shirt,' a rough-edged voice said above her head, sending a shiver of awareness down her spine. 'Save time on the introductions.'

Her gaze lifted to where he was leaning casually on the banister, her breath catching. Did he look sexier than he had the last time? How was that possible? Before she could open her mouth, he turned and disappeared, leaving her to make her way up the stairs and peek through several doors until she found him again. It was beginning to feel as if she'd spent half her life looking for him.

'I have the papers you requested.'

Swiping a cloth over his large hands, he ignored her and began staining the carved piece of wood laid out on a workbench in front of him.

'It's a list of personal assets and properties.'

'You'd think I'd know that if I requested them.'

'You didn't request them?' Not that she'd been there when the call came in, but Carrie on the front desk was normally pretty reliable when it came to—

'Stalking me again?'

'I have *never* stalked you.'

'Some guys might be flattered.'

'I don't think your ego needs any help.'

Had she said that out loud? Maybe he hadn't heard her over the echoing music? The corner of his mouth twitched. Oh, he'd heard. Well, as overjoyed as she was to be a source of amusement to him…

Looking for somewhere to set the file down, her gaze fell on a heavy bed with ornate scrollwork on the posts and a huge headboard carved with curling leaves and branches; incredibly lifelike birds and squirrels were scattered at random intervals. It was practically a work of art. Olivia glanced sideways at him as dense, dark lashes lifted and his intense gaze locked with hers.

The temperature in the room jumped several degrees, a bead of moisture trickling into her cleavage. The woman immediately wanted him to lick the same path it had taken. Even the professional's mouth was dry.

'Did you make that?' She waved the file in the general direction of the bed.

'Showing an interest in what I do the next step in your plan, is it?'

She had to know. 'Are you this judgemental with everyone or have I been singled out for special attention?'

'You want my special attention, sweetheart, all you got to do is ask.'

Shaking her head, Olivia wondered why she was surprised. She should be getting used to it by now, and the accompanying reaction from her body when she realised she was standing within a few feet of evidence he was *good with his hands*.

'You can leave the file.'

He was dismissing her after she'd trekked halfway across the city in temperatures the equivalent of the face of the sun? Olivia didn't think so. Not till they'd cleared up a few things.

'Mr Clayton.'

'Blake.'

'If I'm going to work with you—'

'Work with me. Hmm.' He dropped the brush in the can of wood stain. 'Still haven't figured it out, have you?'

'Figured what out?'

'Didn't you go to some fancy law school to learn all this stuff?' He wiped his hands on the cloth again.

'All *what* stuff?'

'Stuff like who calls the shots.' Tossing the cloth aside, he continued holding her gaze. 'You won't be working *with* me. If I hire you, you'll work *for* me.'

Technically true, but she could argue a technicality. 'I'm employed by—'

'Seriously—' the corner of his mouth tugged again '—consider the T-shirt.'

'*They* pay my salary.'

'And Warren Enterprises pays *them*. Way I figure it—since I've just been handed the keys to the kingdom—that means *I* pay you.'

Not until he signed the papers, he didn't.

'So if I'm stepping up to the plate—' a potent smile began to form on his lips '—you get to be at my beck and call, day and night. I holler, you come a-runnin'.'

Summoning the professional demeanour expected of an employee of one of Manhattan's most respected law firms, Olivia stopped herself from running through the endless possibilities involved with being at his beck and call, day and *night*.

Wait a minute. She was playing messenger girl so he could prove a point? Her eyes narrowed. 'Trust me when I tell you I'm not paid anywhere near enough for that kind of service. I'm good at what I do, Mr Clayton. That's why I'm here. I can work *with* you, represent Warren Enterprises' best interests and ensure a smooth transition for you to head of the company. But I'm not going to bring you coffee, I'm not going to jump when you snap your fingers—' she stepped across the room and set the file down beside him '—and I'm not a messenger.'

The slow hand clap started when she was halfway across the room. 'You practice that on the way over?'

Olivia kept going, the words 'justifiable homicide' jumping into her head. She was almost at the door when a large hand captured her elbow, causing her to jerk in surprise. She swung round. She was a heartbeat away from allowing the training of her former career to kick in before she realised where she was and who he was. Horrified by what she might have done, she took an immediate step back, bumping her spine into the doorframe.

She closed her eyes. 'Please tell me you didn't stain this doorframe before I got here.'

When she opened her eyes again, he was setting a palm on the wood beside her neck. Immediately glancing at her one remaining escape route, she watched another large palm flatten on the wall beside her waist. Like it or not, she wasn't going anywhere. Not without hurting him.

'Nice speech,' he commented.

'I meant every word of it,' she said with a lift of her chin, trying desperately to ignore the erratic thudding of her heart. One man should *not* be that breathtakingly gorgeous up close. She took a deep breath and stifled a moan. He absolutely shouldn't smell that good.

For a second she felt a little bit dizzy. She could really do with some air that wasn't filled with testosterone. Everything around him contracted and went fuzzy again, leaving her unable to focus on anything but him. Her gaze went to the full lip she was so attracted to—the one she wanted to kiss, lick with the tip of her tongue, suck and maybe even nibble a little.

When had she got so sexually frustrated? She tried to remember the last time she'd been on a date—the kind with the remotest possibility of ending in great sex.

Well, *that* was depressing.

'If you're not up to the task, maybe I need to find another lawyer.'

Thank you! It was exactly how she needed him to be. If he added charm—or, worse still, seduction—to an already potent mix, she would be in deep, deep trouble.

Not to mention naked. *Fast.*

'For the record, Mr Clayton, underestimating me is a bad idea.' And she wasn't kidding about that. Thanks to her former profession, she could have him flat on his face on the floor in less than ten seconds and when it came to her present occupation— 'I've been assigned to the Warren accounts since I joined the firm. I know the company inside out and back to front. You won't find anyone more qualified than me.'

He frowned. 'You worked for Charlie?'

'I met him.' She softened a fraction at the mention of the father he'd lost. 'But I didn't work with him.'

'For him,' he corrected.

'*With* him,' Olivia argued. 'That's how we do things at the firm: we work *with* our clients. It's a long-term partnership based on mutual trust and common goals.'

'I'm not looking to get married, sweetheart. I'm looking for someone to do what I tell them to do when I tell them to do it. Is that a problem for you?'

'You tell me to jump, I ask how high?'

'Works for me...'

Over. Her. Dead. Body.

Her breath caught as his head lowered. *What was he doing?* When he stilled, his face inches away from hers, every fibre of her body ached with an almost crippling desire to be kissed. How could she dislike him and want him so badly at the same time? Maybe the heat was getting to her. They said people did things they wouldn't normally do during a heatwave. Olivia just wished she was the kind of girl who hid behind excuses when they did something stupid.

'What's wrong, Liv?' he asked in a low, excruciatingly sensual rumble. 'Not good at taking orders?'

'Depends what they are,' she replied in an equally low voice. And what they were doing at the time.

Don't go there, the professional warned the woman.

When a knowing smile began to form in his eyes, she frowned, swiftly getting back to business with, 'I won't do anything illegal.'

'Unless I'm mistaken, a big part of your job would be to make sure *I* don't.'

'Whatever trouble you get into away from Warren Enterprises isn't my concern.'

'I'll keep that in mind when I'm only allowed to make one phone call.'

The man had no shame. Raised on a diet of discipline and obeying the letter of the law, Olivia had never considered herself the kind of woman who would be attracted to a bad boy but apparently she'd been wrong. Who knew?

'I assume I can't schedule any meetings north of the border.' She analysed his reaction with a tilt of her head.

'Probably best not,' he replied without giving anything away.

She sighed heavily. 'Is this how it's going to be every time we try to have a discussion?'

'That's what we're doing, is it?'

She aimed a narrow-eyed glare at him.

'So what's it to be?' he asked. 'We got a deal?'

'I'm not going to come running when you holler.'

'Where's the fun in that?'

'I think you'll find it would be more fun for one of us than it would for the other.' Inwardly groaning at the fact she was encouraging him, she moved on to the next point. 'I have no problem working outside office hours, but you can't call me in the middle of the night.' Her errant gaze dipped to his tempting lower lip. 'There are boundaries I'm not willing to cross.'

'Like never mix business with pleasure—you have a rule on that, right?'

As it happened, yes, she did. Olivia *liked* rules. It was part of the reason she loved the law so much. A single set of rules for everyone to follow, there for the protection of all. It was an even playing field and she was less likely to mess up as badly as she had before if she worked within the boundary lines.

'Yes,' she replied.

'Why am I not surprised?' He shook his head. 'But you're still not getting it. I'm not questioning your capabilities. If they sent you to deal with this, I'm sure you're up to the task.'

Then what—?

'But here's how it's gonna be, sweetheart. The only advice you get to give me is law-related—you don't question my decisions unless it's something that might get me prosecuted, sued, or both—and there's no First Amendment for free speech in this arrangement. We clear on that?'

Olivia blinked in surprise as the woman inside her purred like a cream-filled cat. Suddenly she understood why Charles Warren had chosen him as his heir. He didn't sound like a man who didn't want the responsibility of the legacy that had been left to him; he sounded like a man taking charge and more than up to the task.

It was exactly how Jo had described him: *sexy as sin.*

Who *was* this man? Tilting her head, she looked at him more closely. Her curious gaze whispered over his face, taking in every detail from the crease lines at the corners of his dark eyes that suggested he laughed more often than she'd had evidence of thus far to the small scar on his chin her fingertips itched to touch while she asked how he'd got it.

'*Liv—*' his deep voice held what sounded like an edge of warning, forcing her gaze back up '—we clear?'

Right. Negotiations. *Focus.*

'No middle of the night phone calls,' she insisted.

She could do the maths. Her dreams of late plus that voice on the other end of a phone line multiplied by the never-ending heatwave they'd been experiencing equalled the road to insanity.

'Not unless it's something I need an answer to right away,' he allowed.

'You holler expecting me to come running, I'll tell you to go to hell.'

'I'll keep that in mind.'

Olivia nodded firmly. 'Then we're clear.'

'Good. I want to go through personal assets first. Can you handle that area?'

She nodded again.

'We'll start looking at the properties on the list you brought me tomorrow.'

Another nod, then, without warning, the tip of his thumb brushed back a strand of hair from her neck, the light graze of work-roughened skin sending a sharp jolt through her body that tightened her abdomen.

'Now that's settled,' he said in a seductively rough rumble as the backs of his fingers trailed lazily over the sensitive skin below her ear, 'I think we should discuss your rule...'

What rule? She had a rule?

Blake watched the movement of his fingers, his head lowering. 'How set in stone would you say that is?'

Oh, this was bad. This was *really* bad.

It felt good.

Breathing ragged, pulse erratic, her heart threatening to beat a hole in her chest, Olivia felt the hand on the wall slide to her waist. The fingers on her neck moved to her nape as his gaze focused intently on her mouth.

'Blake...' Her voice was thick, the unspoken plea caught somewhere between *stop* and *don't stop.*

The tip of his thumb brushed against her jaw as his gaze lifted to search her eyes and a slow smile began to form on the sensual curve of his mouth. 'That's a step in the right direction.'

'What is?'

'My name. It's the first time you've used it.'

It was?

'Say it again,' he demanded, his smile growing. 'Practice makes perfect.'

The sparkle of amusement in his eyes snapped her to her senses. What was she doing? He wasn't caught up in the moment the way she was. He knew *exactly* what he was doing. Worse still, he knew what it was doing to *her.*

Never in all her born days had she been more tempted to play the tease and hand out a little payback. But since she was pretty sure playing up to him would give him exactly what he wanted…

As if the wall would magically move and place some distance between them if she just pushed hard enough, Olivia leaned back and fought through the fog of residual desire and a rapidly descending red mist to form a lightning-fast list of defensive moves she could use without causing any lasting damage. It didn't matter that he was bigger and stronger than she was—she'd been trained for that. Step one: verbal warning.

She opened her mouth and sucked in a sharp breath.

'Hey, Anders, we're going to the deli,' a voice called, making her aware the music had stopped. 'You coming?'

'Did I mention I owe you one for my new call sign?' He stepped back and responded with, 'Right behind you.'

Olivia frowned as she exhaled. He couldn't leave. They weren't done yet.

'We'll pick this up in the morning—nine a.m.—first place on your list.' To her complete astonishment and immeasurable irritation, he flashed a grin that knocked her on her ear. He even had the unmitigated gall to add a wink before telling her, 'I'll bring my own coffee.'

There. Weren't. Words.

Olivia followed him through the door and down the hall. 'Mr Clayton—'

'We're back to Mr Clayton again?'

'This is a professional relationship, nothing more.'

'Don't remember agreeing to that.'

'As I said, there are lines I won't cross.'

'Lack of adventure noted.'

'It's got nothing to do with a lack of adventure.' She

followed him down the first flight of stairs. 'You seem to be under the impression—'

'That you're attracted to me?'

'I am *not*—' Her breath caught when he turned without warning and she found herself looking directly into his eyes again, up close and personal.

How did that keep happening?

Placing large hands on lean hips, he nodded firmly. 'Add lying to me to the list: *don't do it.*'

'I wasn't—'

'Yes, you were.'

Well, yes, she was, but he couldn't know that. What part of dealing with a lawyer hadn't he got? Did he think she couldn't look into his sensationally dark, fathomless eyes and conceal what she wanted? How did he think lawyers negotiated with other lawyers?

She lifted her chin. 'You're not the first difficult client I've worked with, Mr Clayton.'

'Blake. And worked *for*...'

The question slipped out before she could stop it. 'Does this tactic work for you with women?'

'This one isn't?'

'No.'

'You sure about that?'

Oh, he was annoying.

The corners of his mouth twitched with barely suppressed amusement as he dropped his hands to his sides. 'You want something to eat before you head back?'

'No.' She faltered, remembering the manners drummed into her from an early age. 'Thank you.'

'Then I'll see you tomorrow.' He flashed another grin as he turned away. 'Try not to miss me too much.'

Olivia shook her head as he jogged down the second flight of stairs. The man was unbelievable. But if he thought he had the upper hand, he was mistaken. She could maintain her professional decorum under trying circumstances. No way was she screwing up two careers inside a decade. Henceforth, she was enacting a strictly at arm's length policy. No encouraging him through verbal engagement, no rising to the bait—even if she had to bite her damn tongue off—and if he ever got close enough to do the whole addle-her-senses thing he was so good at…

Yeah, she really couldn't let that happen again.

Continuing down the stairs, she allowed herself a brief foray into fantasy where she could hand out a little quid pro quo. In that universe she would have the same effect on him as he had on her. She would play on it, winding him tight, getting him so hot and hard for her, he'd *beg*—

She took a deep breath and blew it out with puffed cheeks. Since that train of thought wasn't helping any, she started looking for loopholes in his stupid rules as she made her way back to the office. Women like her didn't have hot, steamy casual sex with men like him—even if they were tempted.

Really, *really* tempted…

CHAPTER THREE

BLAKE walked around the vast expanse of space that had been one of Charles Warren's last purchases. The view of Central Park's lush green treetops, rolling lawns and duck ponds beneath the sharp contrast of the Manhattan skyline was spectacular, there was no denying that. But could he see himself living there?

Hell, no.

'Pretty amazing, isn't it?'

Olivia followed him around with a file cradled against her breasts and the same transparent enthusiasm as a realtor looking to make a sale. It wouldn't last. After several days in her company one-on-one, Blake knew she started the day in a better mood than she ended it. He liked to think he'd had something to do with that.

'Amazing would be one word.' Turning towards her, he pushed his hands into the pockets of his jeans. 'Little over the top, don't you think?'

Everything about the place had been over the top since they arrived on the red-carpeted steps outside one of New York's most prestigious landmark hotels. A liveried doorman had touched the peak of his cap as they stepped into the revolving doors. The manager had met them in the foyer, shaken Blake's hand and practically fallen over himself to make it clear he could get anything from anywhere at a moment's notice. There had even been maids in traditional uniforms who magically scurried out of sight when the doors to the penthouse were opened. Blake had hated every moment.

Even while he stood inside three floors of some of the largest square footage known to Manhattan apartment-kind, he could feel the walls closing in on him.

'It's…opulent…' she replied after some thought.

'Opulent would be another word.'

Looking at the long sofas placed at right angles to a massive wood-burning stove, he took his hands out of his pockets, sat down, and stretched his arms along the cushions at the back. As he set his feet on the glass coffee table, he saw Olivia frown in disapproval before she controlled her expression.

'You could redecorate.'

'What would you change?' he asked, idly swaying his feet from side to side. When she frowned again, he stopped the movement and stifled a smile. There were times she made it too easy for him.

'It's not mine to change.'

'If it was…'

Her gaze flickered briefly to his, then away. She'd been doing that a lot. Different sides of an elevator, more than an arm's length away when they were walking, subtle side-steps if he moved any closer—he'd noticed them all and each and every one had either amused or bugged him to varying degrees.

'I'm afraid that doesn't fall under the remit of my professional opinion,' she replied as she wandered around the room.

'Humour me.'

'I don't think that's in my job description either.' Smiling sweetly, she turned to face him; she decided several items of expensive furniture provided a safe distance between them.

'Kills you to even think about breaking a rule, doesn't it?'

'Your rules, not mine.'

Seemed to Blake she'd been pretty damn close to breaking a rule when he'd been inches away from kissing her. But since thinking about reminding her had the same effect on his body it always did, he lifted his feet and pushed upright. 'May as well check out the bedrooms.'

'I'll wait here.'

'Where I lead, you follow.'

She lagged behind more noticeably on the second floor than she had when he'd looked at the large kitchen with its black marble counters or through the rounded bay windows overlooking the reflecting pool and plantings in the plaza's courtyard. She remained silent while Blake threw open random doors to increasingly decadent bedrooms and mosaic-tiled bathrooms; each and every room possessed a chandelier whether it needed one or not.

Feet sinking into the deep-piled carpeting in the master bedroom, he walked across to the giant bed, sat on the edge and bounced a couple of times before looking to where Olivia watched warily from the door.

'Take a seat.' He patted the covers. 'If we're lucky we might see a camel before the harem gets back.'

'It's not that bad.'

He held her gaze and waited.

'Okay,' she admitted reluctantly. 'Maybe it's a *little* over the top.'

It was the kind of understatement the place could use in Blake's opinion. Restless again, he walked to the windows. 'Remind me how many properties I own in Manhattan.'

'Fifteen.'

'Current value of this place?'

'Fifty-three million...give or take...'

When he looked over his shoulder—brows raised in disbelief—she cut a smile loose, distracting him from the ridiculous price tag with how it lit her up from inside. She should smile like that more often, he thought, forcing his gaze to look out of the window again. For a moment, when her reflection came into focus on the glass, he watched her looking at him. Her smile faded as she bit her lower lip and checked him out from head to toe. She did that a lot. It was her 'tell' in the game they were playing, his way of knowing she was bluffing when she'd claimed she wasn't attracted to him.

'Sell it,' he said firmly, forcing his gaze from her reflection to the clear blue sky above the city. 'There's a private jet on that list, isn't there?'

'Three of them,' she replied with resignation. 'Let me guess, you want to sell them, too.'

'Explain to me why I need three private jets.'

'Senior executives use them to—'

'Join the Mile High Club?' His gaze sought her reflection again. 'Understandable. The restrooms on commercial airlines can be a tad tight when it comes to wriggle room.'

She sighed. 'You're very cynical when it comes to people with money. Isn't that going to be a problem when you look in the mirror?'

It had taken long enough. Blake bit back a smile, 'Is that an opinion?'

Pressing her lips together, she breathed deep, striving for what remained of the patience he'd been purposefully testing. 'I don't see why we're visiting these properties if you're going to sell everything.'

'And now she's questioning my decisions...'

'Fine,' she replied. 'That's eight properties and three private jets, bringing your running total to approximately one hundred million dollars.'

Resisting the addition of a *congratulations*, she opened her file, made a note, snapped it shut and left the door. Blake turned away from the window and followed her into the hall, his mood improving by the second.

'Hold off on the sale of a jet. Apart from the Mile High possibilities, we might need it when we go to look at the overseas properties.'

She swung around to face him. 'You never said anything about taking trips overseas.'

'Is your passport out of date?'

'That's not the point.' She frowned as he closed the gap between them. 'I can't drop everything and go jetting around the world with you so you can spend five minutes looking at each of the places you're planning on selling.'

'Who says I'm planning on selling them?'

'Aren't you?'

'Depends.'

'On what?' She arched a brow as she looked into his eyes. 'Whether or not they look like something thrown together from a tsar's yard sale?'

The corners of his mouth twitched. 'Meaning you think it's more than a *little* over the top. Could *you* live here?'

'No,' she admitted reluctantly.

'What would you do with it?'

She sighed again. 'Sell it to someone who could.'

'Uh-huh.' He nodded.

When he stepped into her personal space, she lifted the file and hugged it against her breasts like a shield. Glancing away, she held her breath for a moment before sizing him up from the corner of narrowed eyes. 'You want to look at every property, no matter where it is?'

'Maybe.'

'Do you have any idea how many properties you own overseas?'

'Is there a prize if I get it right?'

'It could take *weeks* to visit all those countries.'

'On a tight schedule, are we?'

Cocking her head, she came back with, 'You tell me.'

Closing his thumb and forefinger over the file, Blake tugged and watched her reaction when the instinctive tightening of her hold caused the backs of his fingers to brush against the skin between the lapels of her jacket. She sucked in a sharp breath, her eyes darkening a shade. But when he smiled in response, she let go of the file and lifted her chin in defiance.

The woman had a unique way of looking at him: As if she was hinting heavily she could drop him to his knees with very little effort and he was lucky he was still upright. It was one heck of a turn-on for a man whose personal preference ran to strong-willed women. They were right up there with women whose confidence in their abilities added to their sex appeal and who knew what they wanted in the bedroom and weren't afraid to demand it. She'd find he could be very accommodating with the latter. He might not stick around long enough for anything to get complicated but when he took a lover there was no question in her mind he was one hundred per cent with her.

He took a great deal of pride in that.

Turning his upper body to make room, he opened the file and pretended to read the contents. 'You want to tell me what the real problem is?'

'Meaning?'

The way Blake saw it, it was one of two things. 'Either you hate the idea of taking an all expenses paid trip around the world—' which didn't seem likely '—or you hate the idea of taking that trip *with me*.' Closing the file, he turned and lowered his voice. 'Worried about breaking your mixing business with pleasure rule if you spend more time with me?'

'No.'

'No?' he challenged softly.

While tapping the spine of the file with the palm of his hand, his gaze wandered over her face. The arch of her brows, the length of darkly spiked lashes, the sparkle of warning in her eyes—she really was something.

'There's a reason that rule exists,' she said tightly.

'Office romance gone bad?'

'That would be none of your business.'

'Married, huh?'

There was a small noise that almost sounded like a growl. 'You are the most—'

'I've been told.'

'You really don't care what people think, do you?'

It was said as if it was a completely alien idea to her, something Blake found telling. Appearances mattered, judging by the number of times she straightened the endless selection of suits that had to be *hell* to wear during the heatwave they were experiencing, but it went deeper than fashion. Her personality was adjusted according to the demands of her profession, even if it meant suppressing what she thought and felt—the latter explaining why she'd been able to follow his rules for as long as she had when Blake wouldn't have lasted five minutes.

'Does it matter?' he asked.

'If you care?'

'What people think…?'

She frowned. 'Yes.'

'Why?'

Long lashes flickered as she looked over his shoulder and considered her answer. 'Because the attitude we project tends to influence the attitude we receive in return.'

A hint aimed at him, no doubt.

Blake laid the file against her breasts when she looked into his eyes again. 'Then maybe you should try being nicer to me.'

Her mouth opened then closed, her lips pressed together to stop herself from saying what she thought.

Time for a little prodding. 'Know what I think?'

She took the file. 'I'm sure I'm about to.'

'I think frustration makes you testy.'

The hand holding the file snapped down to her side. 'If I'm testy it might have more to do with the fact you're hardly the easiest person in the world to work with.'

'Work *for*.' When she turned and headed for the stairs, Blake followed at a leisurely pace. 'You're really struggling with that part of the arrangement, aren't you?'

'I'm not used to winging it,' she announced in a voice that echoed down the hallway. 'Did it occur to you if you told me what it is you're thinking of doing with all this money, I could plan ahead?'

'Lack of organisation isn't the reason you're frustrated, sweetheart. You don't want to think about kissing me. Trouble is, you can't *stop* thinking about it. You're angry. Probably blame me for it…'

She spun around to face him at the top of the stairs. '*You* are the most arrogant man I have ever met.'

'You should get out of the office more.'

'This attitude won't help in the boardroom.'

Since he didn't plan on ever stepping into one it was a moot point. Blake smiled a slow smile at how close she was to losing her temper. It was about time. If he'd been her, she'd have strangled him by now.

'Don't do that,' she warned.

His smile grew. 'Do what?'

'You know exactly what you're doing.' She wrinkled her nose. 'And trust me when I tell you, you *really* don't want to play this game with me.'

'Don't want to like me, do you?'

'If I did, you wouldn't be making it easy,' she muttered. Scowling, she turned a little too quickly. Her eyes widened when the toe of her shoe slipped over the edge of the top stair and her heel caught. The file dropped from her hand as she swung her arms out to her sides for balance, grasping for a railing just out of her reach.

Before she fell, Blake snagged an arm around her waist and hauled her round against him.

Grabbing handfuls of his shirt, she uttered a breathless, 'Thank you.'

'You're welcome.' He smiled. When she tried to move he tightened his arm. 'Give it a minute.'

If her heart was thundering as loudly as his it would do them both good. He'd never have forgiven himself if she'd tumbled headlong down two flights of stairs. But as her breathing slowed, his concern, tempered by relief, was replaced with something more potent.

She blinked once, twice; the fingers holding his shirt loosened and her palms flattened as if she couldn't stop herself touching him.

Then her gaze lifted.

With her guard down, he was shown how truly expressive her eyes could be. Curiosity threaded with need, confusion tangled up in desire—and those were just the things he could recognise. Everything she was feeling danced in the light of a blue flame he was drawn to with the same compulsion he felt to draw air into his lungs. Did she have any idea what she was willing him to do when she looked at him like that? The effect it had on his body when she had her hands on him? He searched her eyes for a hint of power in the knowledge, feeling marginally better when he couldn't find it. If she knew, he'd be in trouble.

As her palms slid across his chest and down his arms, he tensed, unable to stop the telltale sign from happening; it was almost as if part of him wanted her to know. Her gaze lowered as she felt it happen, hands sliding down to his elbows, her mesmerized expression suggesting she was watching what she was doing as if it was some kind of out-of-body experience.

Blake studied the soft sheen of hair against her forehead before lowering his chin and looking at her hands where they rested against the rolled up sleeves of his shirt. Such small, fine-boned hands, such a light touch, but he could feel the effect of it scorching into his veins, transforming his blood to the same consistency as lava: thick, heavy and fiery-hot.

Damn, they were going to be good together.

When their gazes lifted, she focused on his mouth.

'Do it,' he demanded in a huskier voice than he'd have preferred.

'Do what?' she asked in a thick voice.

'Kiss me.'

She shook her head.

'You're thinking about it.'

'No, I'm not,' she lied.

Moving his fingertips in slow, soothing circles on her back, Blake silently willed her to forget whatever was holding her back. 'If you spent less time trying to pretend this isn't here we might get along better.'

'I don't want—'

'Yes, you do.' Raising a hand, he used the backs of his fingers to brush her hair off her cheek. 'You've been thinking about the kiss that never happened.' Just like he had. 'Wondering what it would have felt like if it had…'

Why should he be the only one tortured by it?

Turning his hand, he traced his fingertips over her jaw to the sensitive skin below her ear. She leaned her head towards her shoulder in response, dutifully arching her neck to allow him access as her eyelids grew heavy. Her body couldn't hide the truth any more than his could.

'Don't you want to find out, Liv?' He dipped his head and saw the lift of her chin bring her mouth closer to his.

'You'll have to fire me first.'

'I'm not going to fire you,' he answered in the same husky-edged tone as before. 'You'll have to quit.'

'I'm no quitter,' she replied, an incredibly sensuous smile curling her lips.

'Neither am I.'

When she breathed deep and exhaled on a hum of what sounded distinctly like pleasure, he stifled a groan. The slow slide of her lower lip between her teeth, the hooded gaze she had focused on his mouth—she was testing him, wasn't she? If she was, it was a test he was failing.

Sensing the balance of power shifting, he took a short breath. 'Word of warning, sweetheart—I never said anything about making it impossible for you *not* to kiss me.'

There was a flash of light in her eyes.

'I think…' she said in an intimate tone as one of her hands slid back up his arm, '*you…*'

Blake's body tightened with anticipation as she angled her head and moved closer.

'Should…' A fingernail trailed tantalisingly over his skin where the collar of his shirt touched his neck; her palm flattened as she lowered her hand to his chest. 'Keep this apartment…'

What?

Lifting her chin, she brought her mouth closer to his. She looked up at him and informed him, 'The ceilings are just about high enough for your head to fit in here.'

Fixing him with a heavy gaze that said *gotcha*, she leaned back against his arm and smiled tightly. 'You might want to let me go now. I'd hate to have to hurt you.'

Judging by her expression, he doubted she'd hate it that much. But conceding a hand didn't mean the game was over. Releasing her, he stepped to the side and bent down to retrieve the file. 'What next?'

She arched a brow as she tugged her jacket straight.

'On the list.' He waved the file back and forth.

'Another penthouse…'

'Any chance this one doesn't have a guy in a top hat at the door?'

'I doubt it.' She reached for the file.

When she tried to take it from him, Blake held on, waiting for her to look into his eyes before he smiled meaningfully.

'We're not done.'

She lifted her chin, a smile sparkling in her eyes and hovering on her lips.

'I know.'

Relinquishing the file, he turned towards the stairs and held out an arm. Suddenly the next few weeks didn't feel like such a chore to him any more. He should probably thank her for that. As it was, he would have to up his game. The way he saw it, by the time he was done she was either going to kiss him or kill him.

He smiled as she stepped past him. 'Mind the step…'

Olivia rolled her eyes.

CHAPTER FOUR

BREATHING deep, Olivia mentally continued banging her forehead on the edge of the breakfast counter.

Stupid, stupid, stupid…

She should never have told her friends how tough she was finding it dealing with Blake. They'd talked about little else ever since. There was no escape from him now.

'I think you should quit working with him,' Jess said over the rim of her mug. 'If you're on a diet, it doesn't make sense to hang out by the dessert cart.'

Jo cut to the chase. 'Apart from the fact you work with him, what's the problem? Run it past us.'

'It would just be sex.' Olivia shrugged.

Jess stared at her as if she'd lost her mind, 'Not seeing that as a problem unless it's really *bad* sex.'

Nope. She was pretty sure it would fall into the rock-her-world category, judging by her response to his most recent tactics. Since she'd started slipping up and playing him at his own game, he'd pulled out the big guns, breaking down her defences with his irreverent sense of humour and targeting her biggest weakness with his obvious skills in the art of seduction. He was, without doubt, the most annoying man she'd ever met but at the same time there was something almost roguishly charming about—

Jo narrowed her eyes as she saw Olivia smile. Olivia

avoided her gaze and cleared away her breakfast things. 'I've got to go. I have calls to make before I meet Blake at Union Square.'

'There doesn't automatically have to be a consequence for letting go,' her friend said from the bedroom door.

Grabbing her jacket and her briefcase, Olivia pushed her feet into her favourite pair of heels. 'There's no point letting go with a guy like him.'

'They don't all have to be keepers.'

'I'm not looking for a keeper.'

'Doesn't mean you don't recognise keeper qualities when you see them… Great sex is on everyone's wish-list.' She shrugged. 'I say go for it if this guy does it for you. How often does *that* happen?'

They both knew the answer to that.

'It's about time you had some fun…'

Blake most definitely fit the bill in that department. There wasn't anything about him that yelled steady, stable or long-term. Worse came to worst, she'd already vowed she'd do her damnedest to make sure he caved before she did. If there was one thing that bugged her more than arrogance, it was smugness.

'Know what I'd do if I was in your shoes?' Jo asked.

'Shoes are off limits. Don't make me do an inventory.'

Linking their arms at the elbow, her friend walked her to the door of their apartment. 'I'd cut my inner bad girl loose and make it impossible for *him* not to kiss *me*.'

Except the problem wasn't about kissing or not being kissed by him. Maybe—just once in her twenty-eight years—she should have fun with a man who could take her on with a distinct chance of winning: a trait she'd long since recognised in Blake. If anything, with her background, it would be freeing as hell.

'It's okay, you know.'

'What is?' She blinked.

'Letting go a little and having fun. You can't stay shut off for ever, Liv. Not when you have so much to give.'

Despite the fact she wasn't sure she was ready to take that step, Olivia hugged Jo before heading down the hall to the elevator. If she let go and allowed herself to get emotionally involved again there was a danger she might open a door it had taken a long time to close. She had an all-or-nothing personality but, with a great deal of time and effort, she liked to think she'd learnt to control her emotions the way she should have a lot earlier. It was better that way, safer for all concerned. Unfortunately, at times it was also something else…

Lonely.

And now she was starting her day even more in need of fun than before. *That would help.*

'I'm starting to think you sleep in a suit.'

'What makes you think I wear anything in bed?' Walking along the busy sidewalk, she glanced sideways at him while yet another inner bad girl comment slipped off the tip of her errant tongue.

'Understandable in this weather,' his deep, rough-edged voice replied. 'Dial up the air con, wait for that first whisper of cool air on your skin as you kick off the covers.' He nodded. 'I'm a big fan of sleeping naked.'

Great, now she'd spend the rest of the day thinking about him lying naked in bed—waiting for her—watching while she dialled up the air conditioning and came back to join him so they could pick up where they'd left off.

She was beginning to feel like General Custer with advance knowledge of how the battle would turn out.

'A cold shower would help,' she muttered.

Blake took a step closer when she stopped walking,

leaning in to speak in a low, seductive tone that tested what remained of her resolve. 'Turn up the temperature some, we could take one together.'

The woman whose needs had been suppressed for entirely too long dipped a hip towards him, lowered her lashes and fixed her gaze on the strong column of his neck. It would be so very easy to set her lips to the tanned skin there. She could work her way up to his strong jawline, whisper in his ear every little detail of the things she wanted him to do to her beneath the running water of that shower. Looking into his eyes, she caught her lower lip between her teeth.

'You say a lot without words.'

'I have two words for you,' she said in a purposely low voice.

'Let's go?' he asked optimistically.

'We're here.' She smiled.

He glanced at the doorway of the large building beside them, his expression changing. 'You sure?'

'Yes.'

'Right.' A muscle tightened in his jaw but, before she could ask what was wrong, he was halfway up the steps.

Inside the grand foyer, he headed for an area filled with comfortable chairs and large pieces of furniture, his back to her—shoulders tense—while Olivia introduced them to the receptionist and asked for the manager.

'How long did he own this place?' he asked when she stood beside him.

Olivia checked the file. 'Eight years.'

'Ms Brannigan, Mr Clayton, I'm Frank Gains, manager of—' He was shaking Olivia's hand when his gaze shifted. 'Blake?'

'Frank.' Blake held out a hand as he turned.

The older man seemed flustered. 'I didn't know.'

'Didn't you?'

'I didn't make the connection. Your name...'

A confused Olivia looked from one to the other. She had absolutely no idea what was going on. Blake nodded curtly as he dropped his arm to his side. When he walked back towards the entrance without saying anything more, she blinked in surprise.

'He's Charles Warren's son?' the manager asked.

She nodded. 'I take it you've met before.'

'His guys did some of our renovations a few years back. It's not easy to find skilled craftsmen these days, especially for an older building. We didn't want to lose the character of the place...'

Ironic as it was, considering how little of it they'd taken up, Olivia thanked him for his time and followed Blake outside. Standing on the sidewalk, she squinted against the bright sunshine, raising her hand to shield her eyes as she scanned the crowd until she found him across the street in Union Square. He was watching a woman dressed as the Statue of Liberty walk by, plastic torch tucked under her arm while she adjusted the foam crown on her head.

His gaze collided with Olivia's as he waited for her to get close enough to hear him say, 'Sell it.'

Not that it was a surprise, but, 'You didn't know, did you? When you took the job there, you didn't know it was your father's hotel.'

He frowned.

'I asked the manager how he knew you.' When he turned away, she followed him. 'You obviously weren't close.'

'Good guess.'

'But he left you everything.'

As they walked into the farmers' market set up at one end of the park, Blake slowed his pace before stopping to look over some of the produce. 'There's very little left of the Warren gene pool. In the end I figure he had a choice between the family bastard and a cousin who's doing time for illegal possession. If it narrows it down for you, I'm not the one wearing an orange jumpsuit.'

Olivia digested the information while he headed for another canopied stall that had caught his interest. The market in a tree-filled Union Square was an orgy for the senses, with plenty to distract the eye, but her mind refused to let go of the opportunity to get answers to some of the questions she'd had before she met him.

'Here.'

She leaned back when he held a small lump of something creamy-coloured in front of her face, 'What is it?'

'Goats' cheese, with honey.'

'I'll pass.'

'That lack of adventure again.' Shaking his head, he popped the sample in his mouth and chewed. 'Your loss.'

Frowning at the comment, she reached out a hand and snagged another sample from the stand, chewing with a smirk before she blinked in surprise.

'Good?'

'Mmm.' She nodded appreciatively as she swallowed, falling into step beside him as he headed for the next stand. 'Did you know you were his heir?'

'Did it look like I knew when you told me?' He stopped and turned towards her. 'Try this one.'

Olivia accepted the sample without protest, her grimace making the corners of his mouth twitch.

'No?'

'What *was* that?' She frowned at the produce on the stand in disgust.

'Celeriac.'

Taking a mental note of the offence against taste buds,

she followed him to the next stand while trying to scrape the taste off her tongue with her teeth, 'How well did you know him?'

'Does it matter?'

'It's unusual for someone to leave everything they own to a complete stranger.'

'If you say so.' He turned around. 'Here.'

'What is it?' Her eyes narrowed, the celeriac memory causing suspicion.

Blake twirled the sprig of small green leaves between his thumb and forefinger as he held it closer to her mouth. 'You tell me.'

When he brushed one of the leaves over the parting of her lips, she lifted her arm and wrapped her fingers around his to still the movement. A jolt travelled up her arm as soon as skin touched skin, instantly tightening her nipples against the suddenly abrasive lace of her bra. Her gaze locked on his as her breath caught. How did he *do* that?

'I've got it,' she said in a low voice.

'When you put your mind to it, yes, you have.'

She fought the need to smile at the compliment.

Raising their hands, he held the sprig of leaves beneath her nose, the backs of long fingers resting lightly against her lips. 'Breathe in.'

'I know what you're doing,' she mumbled as she dropped her hand.

'What is it?'

Six foot three of increasingly irresistible male, but since Olivia assumed he meant the leaves, she breathed in.

'Mint?'

'Close your eyes.'

'Why?'

When the movement of her lips became a caress against his fingers, his gaze darkened. 'Just do it, Liv.'

Concerned she might give in to the temptation to kiss him if he kept looking at her with an intensity that made it feel as if he were absorbing her into him, Olivia closed her eyes. Theoretically, if she couldn't see him she could pretend he wasn't there. If it wasn't for the touch of his warm fingers against her lips, the scent she found even more addictive with the addition of a hint of mint and the fact she could almost *feel* the air crackling between them.

Somewhere inside her head a white flag was waving.

'Keep them closed.' The rumble of his rough voice resonated through her body, echoing in a hollow place inside her, the existence of which had been denied for a long time.

He really did do it for her.

'Open your mouth.'

While her imagination ran riot with erotic thoughts of him issuing a similar set of demands in a more intimate setting, she took a short breath, opened her mouth and tilted her head back. Placing a small sliver of the leaf on her tongue, the tip of his finger lingered on her lower lip, tracing its shape before sliding along her jaw.

A languid smile formed on Olivia's lips as she chewed.

'Chocolate.' She sighed contentedly. She could taste mint-flavoured chocolate. Apart from the fact it removed the bitter taste of celeriac from her mouth—which was thoughtful of him—combined with his touch, it was bliss.

'That good?'

'Mmm.' Swallowing, she slowly ran the tip of her tongue over her lips, rolled them in on themselves and parted them to draw a deeper breath as she opened her eyes.

'I should taste it,' he said roughly.

'You should,' she agreed.

Reaching out, she wrapped her fingers around his wrist, sliding them down over the back of his hand. He took a half-step closer, head lowering as she lifted her chin. *God*, he was tempting. She *really* wanted to kiss him—just once, so she knew what it was like and didn't have to spend the rest of her life wondering—but with a twist of her thumb and forefinger she had her prize. The opportunity was too good to miss as she held the mint up in front of his face and smiled victoriously.

Realisation sparkled into a glint of amusement when his gaze locked with hers. 'Not what I had in mind.'

'Wasn't it?' She batted her lashes innocently.

'No.'

When his fingertips curled around the nape of her neck, Olivia's heart punched against her breastbone.

Kiss me, the woman in her willed breathlessly.

'You're doing it again,' he said roughly.

'Doing what?'

'You know what.'

She did. That it was having such a strong effect on him was empowering. She wanted him. He wanted her. For the first time it felt that simple to Olivia. All she had to do was take one teeny tiny step over the line and—

Kiss me. The words hovered on the tip of her tongue.

Leaning forward, Blake nudged the tip of his nose off hers, the tantalising jut of his lower lip within millimetres of her mouth as her eyelids grew heavy. Another hand lifted to frame her face, thumb brushing her cheek. The long fingers of the hand on her neck flexed into her hair and made her sink back into his touch. She knew he'd played the seduction card to stop her from asking questions he didn't want to answer. Knew it and should have been irritated by it, but she really didn't want him to stop.

'Blake.' She exhaled his name like a plea.

'Do you know what I hear when you say my name?'

It took considerable effort to shake her head. How was

she supposed to fight this? It felt futile, especially when she couldn't summon the energy to try.

He slid his cheek across hers so he could whisper in her ear. 'I hear: *I want you.*'

'Blake—'

'This guy bothering you?' a voice asked loudly.

Olivia stifled a groan. 'You got to be kidding me.' She turned and glared at the man standing beside them as Blake took a step back. 'Slow day for parking violations?'

'I'm on indecent exposure watch—reckoned if I left it another minute, I'd have to arrest you.' He jerked his head towards Blake. 'Who's your friend?'

'Didn't we agree you guys would stop doing this when I left high school?'

'Should I get my notepad out to take his details?'

She sighed heavily. 'This is Blake. He's a client.'

'Really.'

From anyone else it would have been a timely reminder. 'Blake, my brother, John Brannigan.'

'Last name?' Johnnie asked him without blinking.

'Clayton.'

'Uh-huh.' He nodded. 'And how do you spell that?'

'You run a background check on him, I'll kick your ass,' Olivia warned.

'That's assaulting a police officer.'

'Running a background check on every guy you ever see me with is harassment.' She smiled sweetly. 'Don't make me tell Mom.'

'Go right ahead. She'd appreciate a call more than once a month.'

Low blow.

A call came in on the radio attached to his shoulder, *'Unit nineteen, ten fifty-four...'*

It was an echo from her past—one that still had an effect on her, even after six years. Suddenly it was dark; she could feel rain falling, see coffee cups falling into a trash can and hear a voice calling her name. But at least she didn't get nauseous any more. That was something.

'Gotta go.' Her brother looked Blake straight in the eye. 'Be seeing you.'

Letting the latter slide, Olivia took an automatic step forward. 'What happened?'

'You know the ten codes as well as I do.' He backed away, pointing a finger at her. 'Stay out of trouble.'

Shaking her head, she watched him jog across the square until he disappeared. When she looked at Blake she found a familiar glint of amusement in his eyes.

'You have the police codes memorised?'

'They were funny about that at the academy.' She checked her watch. 'We're early for the next viewing; you want to stop and get coffee?'

His brows lifted. 'You were a cop?'

'Yes.'

There was a brief pause, then, 'Makes sense.'

It did? She glanced sideways at him as they walked to the crossing.

'How long were you a cop?'

'Six months.'

'Not cut out for it?'

'Something like that.' Waiting at the kerb for the signal to change, she glanced up at him again. The smile on his face was different from any of the ones she'd seen before. Her eyes narrowed. 'What?'

'New information. I'm absorbing it and trying to get a mental picture.' He nodded. 'The uniform's working for me.'

Olivia rolled her eyes when his smile turned into something more familiar. The man was incorrigible.

As the traffic stopped, he laid a large palm against the inward curve of her spine, leaning closer as they crossed the street. 'Not the only one who clams up when it's something they don't want to talk about, am I?'

'Meaning I should stop asking questions?'

'Some subjects are easier than others,' he allowed, his gaze focused on their destination. When they were standing in front of the coffee shop, the scent of roasting beans rich in the air, he dropped his arm and turned towards her. 'Why do you need to know?'

'Knowing you better might make my job easier.'

'That the only reason, is it?'

Feeling distinctly as if she were crossing an invisible line, Olivia breathed deep and answered honestly. 'No.'

When he stared at her, she tried to find a way of justifying it that made as much sense to her as it would to him. 'It's part of a cop's job to know why people do the things they do. Everyone has a story—you just have to put the pieces together so you can understand it.'

'You're not a cop any more.'

'True, but lawyers are taught the same thing. If it makes you feel any better, I do it with everyone I meet.' Her gaze lowered to the open collar of his white shirt when she found it difficult to look into his eyes.

If she was being completely honest, she would tell him she didn't want to know everyone's story as badly as she needed to know his. But the fact she'd admitted it to herself was the much needed reminder that had been missing in the square when she came so close to kissing him. Giving in to sexual attraction was one thing, caring about him was another and if she knew more than she already did…

Reaching out, she pushed open the door to the coffee shop. 'Of course you have the right to remain silent.'

'Tell me you still have the handcuffs.'

She chuckled softly. 'You'll never know.'

CHAPTER FIVE

THE place was a wreck.

Sidestepping debris, Blake looked up at the broken panes of glass; the beat of several flapping wings echoed around the huge expanse of space as they interrupted the resident wildlife. Most of the second floor had fallen in, as had part of the roof, but he was willing to bet there were some great views of the river from higher ground.

'How sound is the structure?'

'Will need shoring up before we put the second floor back in, but it's not bad.' The man who had met them with the keys stayed with Liv while Blake walked around. 'The details are in the architect plans I brought with me.'

The commercial elevator was shot, but the staircase beside it looked sound enough, barring a few missing steps. Placing a palm on a large wooden crate, Blake bent his knees, twisted his waist and bounced onto the surface, slapping his palms together when he was upright and reaching out a foot to test the first step. When he put weight on it, there was a loud crack.

Liv took a step forward. 'Be careful.'

When he flashed a grin, she rolled her eyes.

Testing each step before he put his full weight on it, he made his way up to what was left of the second floor.

'If you fall and break your neck I'll make sure they put

"terminal stupidity" as the cause of death on the certificate,' she called up to him.

'Feel free to administer mouth-to-mouth,' he called back.

The properties outside Manhattan were looking better already. He'd been right; the view across the river was great from the second floor—area was ripe for development, too. Be nice to have something within a block of the river that wasn't a generic high-rise. Considering how many of them there were, the building had been lucky to survive. When he looked through a gap in the floorboards, he saw Liv peering up at him, her expression a mixture of disapproval and concern. He smiled.

Placing his hands on his hips, he jerked his head in invitation. 'Come on up.'

'I'm good where I am.'

'Where I lead, you follow.'

'Yeah—' there was a short burst of sarcastic laughter '—that's not happening this time.'

'Not good with heights?'

'I have a very long bucket list.'

Making his way across the floor, he stretched tall to see out of the windows on the other side, frowning as he rocked back. View was pretty good from that side too but it was also familiar. He didn't get it. Had it been so damn difficult for his father to talk to him? Considering the envelope he'd been carrying around for longer than he cared to admit, he supposed it had. They'd been one as bad as the other.

The silent admission made him search inside again for a hint of grief or regret. If he was the kind of guy who shared things with others, he might have admitted his biggest fear was that the great vacuum of nothing would expand like a black hole and swallow up the parts of him that still felt alive. Had he felt the same way after his mom died? No. He'd felt relief then. Partly because she was out of pain, partly because it was over and he was free. He'd felt guilty about the latter, but he'd sat on it, tucked it away and pretended it wasn't there. Maybe that was when it had started. By ignoring it instead of dealing with it, the small dark place where he'd buried the things he didn't want to face had quietly grown while he covered up the emptiness with good times, fun, laughter and the kind of freedom of choice he'd never had before.

A hand lifted to his pocket to check the envelope was safe in a reflex born of habit. It was too late to change the past, so what was he doing revisiting it? Why hadn't he told Liv to sell everything and get back to him when it was done? He didn't need to look at it. Now he had. If there were more places he liked the look of he could find himself having to make decisions he hadn't—

'Blake?'

'I'm coming down.'

Fifteen minutes later they were walking in silence to the water taxi and he was holding a cardboard tube in his hand. Slanting a glance at Liv, he found her smiling.

'What?'

'I find it amusing we've looked at millions of dollars' worth of property and this is the first one you've liked.'

'I'm not a millions of dollars' worth of property guy.'

'You are now.'

'I haven't said I'm keeping it.'

'You're thinking about it,' she said brightly. 'That's a step in the right direction.' When he didn't reply, she took a short breath. 'You just need to find your place in this. Give it time, you'll get there.'

'Do I need to remind you about the rule on advice?'

Stopping in front of the taxi landing, she turned towards him. 'What's wrong?'

'What makes you think there's something wrong?'

'You were different when you came back down.'

'Was I?'

'You can talk to me, you know.' She shrugged a shoulder, downplaying the offer with, 'It won't go any further—attorney/client privilege.'

'I've known you two weeks.'

'Is there someone you *can* talk to?' Angling her head, she studied his eyes and blinked in surprise. 'Wow.'

'You don't know me,' he said tightly.

'Does anyone?'

'Don't make this personal, sweetheart. It's not.'

'Fine. You're right. I don't need to know.'

When she turned and walked away, Blake frowned. He hadn't lied to her, hadn't said anything overly harsh, so why did he suddenly feel the need to make amends?

'I'm not going with you.'

She stopped and turned around.

'I live a few blocks from here.'

Jerking his head to the right, he watched her gaze follow the movement and waited for her to put it together. If she'd been quick enough to figure out his reaction to the hotel, he reckoned she was smart enough to work out he hadn't known about the warehouse on his doorstep either. It was getting to the point where it felt as if he should check the ownership on the lease agreement for his apartment.

He'd thought it was a sweet deal at the time.

When awareness entered her eyes, she nodded.

Blake felt some of the tension roll off his shoulders when she didn't push. 'I'll take a look at these plans and let you know my decision.'

'Okay.'

'And, unless I'm mistaken—' he pointed the end of the tube at her '—you've got a party to go to.'

'The benefit.' She nodded again. 'Will you be there?'

He glanced over her shoulder. 'Taxi's coming.'

As it got closer, the yellow and black hull tearing a swathe of white froth on the surface of the water, she remained still, the corners of Blake's mouth tugging in reaction to her inability to leave him.

'*Go.* I'll see you later.'

She clasped the handle of her briefcase in both hands and swung it around her body as she turned away, flashing a bright smile over her shoulder before she sashayed down the dock. Thought he was wrapped around her little finger, didn't she?

Dropping his chin, Blake chuckled as he left. He was going because he owed her; that was all. Knowing him, spending 24/7 with her would bring their relationship to a swift end. And he wasn't ready for that. Not yet.

She owed him for this, *big time.*

'...with the continued support of Warren Enterprises, naturally we hope to see...'

His attention had long since left the continuing conversation between a State Senator, the Mayor and varying executives who surrounded him. They didn't need his full attention for him to follow the gist. Not when he'd decided part of the role of a brand new billionaire was to assume an air of boredom, more interested in the never-ending supply of champagne circulating on round silver platters than anything business-related. Not that it happened too often, but getting drunk suddenly held a lot of appeal to Blake.

Draining his ridiculously fiddly glass, he reached out an arm to set it on a tray as he smiled at the waitress who'd been circling him. 'Don't suppose there's any chance you could get me a good old-fashioned American beer?'

When the bottle arrived, he ignored the accompanying glass, rewarded the waitress with a smile and turned to look at the couples on the dance floor, his gaze seeking the one thing he did find interesting. In a sea of black and white it didn't take much to pick out the shimmering gold highlighted in her hair by surrounding strings of fairy lights, but when the crowd rolled into a different position she disappeared like a ghost. *There.* This time her head turned towards him as long lashes lifted and her gaze locked with his. When the crowd shifted again, he frowned.

Damn that dress.

The rooftop pool deck offered unparalleled views of the Hudson River, Lincoln Centre, Central Park and the city, but even the sight of Manhattan sparkling against the night sky didn't compare to the wondrous sight of the thin-strapped sheath of red silk that left inch upon inch of skin exposed from her shoulders to the dip in her back. Add the way the molten material hugged the curve of her hips, outlined impossibly long legs when she moved and barely skimmed the edges of the small breasts that would fill his palms and—

He ground his teeth together as she waltzed around the crowded dance floor in the arms of a smooth model-type. A couple of years shy of Blake's soon-to-be thirty-three, he'd bet the guy was nowhere near as capable of taking her on. He was batting way out of his league.

Large eyes darkened to pools of midnight-blue by the muted light sought him out again before she focused her attention on her partner as the man led her into another turn. It allowed Blake a momentarily uninterrupted view of the perfection of her back. Desire rolled through him and settled heavily in his groin. He wanted to explore every inch of that skin. He wanted to touch and taste, to bury himself deep and get lost in her, those long legs wrapped around him as she cried out his name, and if that guy looked down the front of her dress *one more time…*

He fought the need to go feral. The guy was holding her too close but Liv didn't seem to mind as much as Blake did, a slither of awareness sliding across his senses when she looked at him from the corner of her eye and smiled. Still thought he was wrapped around her little finger, didn't she? To prove she was wrong, he turned and walked away. She wanted him, she could come find him.

He was leaning on the balcony when she did.

Dangling the neck of the bottle between his fingers, he watched her step up beside him to look over the city.

'Run out of dance partners?'

'Thought I'd get some air…'

As he glanced at her, she tilted her head back, eyes closed and a blissful expression on her face as a light, cooling breeze lifted her hair from her shoulders.

'Mmm,' she moaned. 'This is wonderful.'

Blake counted to ten. He was *not* going to fold first.

Turning ninety degrees, she leaned her elbow on the railing and studied his profile. As her gaze lowered and he felt it every place she looked, both down and back up his body, he ground his teeth together and wondered if she had any idea how thin a line she was treading.

'In case I haven't mentioned it—nice tux.'

Lifting the bottle, he spoke over the rim. 'And I got dressed all on my own.'

'You hate every minute of this, don't you?'

'What gave it away?' He turned his head to look at her, frowning at her expression. 'It's not funny.'

'It's a little bit funny.' She stifled the smile sparkling in her eyes.

'Next time I owe you an apology for something, you're getting flowers like everyone else.'

'I like orchids, rare ones.'

'You'll get daisies and be grateful.'

'I *love* daisies.'

Wouldn't give an inch, would she?

'What is it you hate most?' she asked in a soft voice.

'Where do you want me to start?'

'Pick one.'

'*That*—' he tilted his bottle at the crowd '—isn't a party. At a party—' he leaned towards her and lowered his voice '—people have *fun*.'

'They're having fun.'

'No.' He stood tall again. 'What they're doing is networking and using the auction to demonstrate who has the biggest wallet.'

'Okay, then.' With another slight turn, her shoulder pressed lightly against his upper arm. 'Champagne bottle guy, two o'clock, he looks like he's having fun…'

With a ten minute head start in the crowd-watching department, Blake inclined his head towards her. 'Bad day on the stock market. Drowning his sorrows…'

'Marilyn Monroe lookalike, six o'clock…'

'On the hunt for husband number three, trying to make it look like she knows how to have a good time…'

'Stuck-in-the-eighties guy at eleven o'clock?'

'Celebrating the purchase of a midlife crisis sports car,' Blake said as the man held up a set of keys. 'Using it to score with the woman half his age opposite him who comes from the right breeding stock…'

Laughing, Liv lifted her chin. *'Cynic.'*

'Just telling it how it is, sweetheart.' He winked.

The smile remained in her eyes as she continued looking up at him, lips parting as if she was going to say something then closing as a brief hint of a frown creased her forehead.

'Say it,' he demanded. 'Don't stop to think about it.'

'You really don't want to make that one a rule.'

'Say it.'

'I was just going to say you're doing fine. Everyone has been talking about you.'

Blake bit back the kind of response he would normally have given, taking a deep breath and forcing the truth out of his mouth. 'That doesn't help.'

'Good things,' she reassured him, her gaze slanting up and to the side as she added, 'surprisingly…all things considered…' She smiled mischievously as she looked into his eyes again. 'Some of the women made a lot of highly complimentary comments.'

Lifting his brows, Blake looked over the crowd with more interest. 'Anyone you want to point out?'

'Not particularly.'

The change in her tone made him smile. 'Shame—you could have been my wingman—might have livened things up.'

The second she moved, he turned, stretched his arms out and grasped the railing on either side of her narrow waist. 'They say anything you agreed with?'

'I'm likely to admit that?' She circled a finger in front of his face. 'Head size, remember?'

'How much champagne have you had?'

'Not *that* much.'

'Good.' He leaned closer, angling his face above hers. 'Because I want to discuss your rule again.'

'Now?' Her brows lifted.

'Mmm-hmm—' he nodded firmly '—*now*.'

She peeked over his shoulder. 'Not here.'

'You're saying no one kisses at these things?' Blake took that as confirmation of his appraisal of the 'party'.

'Not if it's someone they work with.'

'Work *for*.'

Setting her palms flat against his chest, she pushed, frowning when he didn't move. 'I can't kiss you here.'

'So when you say "not here", it's not that you're denying you want to kiss me—' which would have been a step in the right direction '—it's that you don't want to kiss me where someone might see you kissing me.'

'I wouldn't have put it that way,' she said a little too defensively for his liking. 'You don't understand.'

'Don't I?' He forced a smile onto his face. 'You want to sneak around for a little midday fun, I'm open to that. You want to act like strangers in public while we get it on behind closed doors, you can forget it.'

'I didn't say that.' She scowled.

'It was implied.' Setting his bottle on a nearby planter, Blake grabbed her hand.

'What are you doing?'

'You're going to dance with me.' He tightened his grip and led them to the dance floor where he turned, hauled her against his chest and wrapped an arm around her waist. 'If you think I'm going to watch you dance with a string of guys under my nose while I pretend there's nothing going on between us, *think again*.'

Incredulity filled her eyes as he began swaying them to the music. 'You think I did that to make you jealous? Oh, you do, don't you? And you're telling me…'

When realisation entered her eyes and she caught her lower lip between her teeth to control a smile, Blake shook his head. 'Oh, no, you don't. You don't get to look happy about it. Not after labelling me a guilty secret.'

'That's not what I said!' She glanced around them. 'Would you *stop* putting words in my mouth?'

The fact she'd lowered her voice so no one could hear didn't help.

'Prove me wrong,' he challenged.

'What?'

'You heard me.'

The look she gave him said he couldn't be serious. 'You want an audience the first time I kiss you? Maybe they should make an announcement so nobody misses it. I know what we could do—we could *auction it*. Someone pays enough money, we could put on quite a show for them. That should make it a party to remember.'

Her eyes sparked with a hint of impending danger. Having waited so long for her to lose her cool, it was a shame he was too pissed at her to appreciate the moment. When she pulled back, he held on, his jaw locked with determination. She wasn't going anywhere.

Without giving him enough time to read her intentions, she relaxed in his arms, angled her head, smiled sweetly and kicked him sharply in the shin.

Lurching forward, he looked up as she told him, 'You can be a real jerk when you want to be.'

His burst of deep laughter caught them both off guard.

After a few moments of gentle swaying—allowing time for the storm to pass—she quietly slipped her hand up his chest and around his neck; her fingertips brushed against the short strands of hair touching his collar.

'You don't get it.'

'Then walk me through it.'

'After the stunt you just pulled?' She raised a brow. 'I don't think so.'

Leaning back, his gaze scanned the crowd. It had been

an overreaction—not that he'd never had one of *those* before—but she deserved better.

'I won't hide,' he heard his voice say. 'Not again.'

The confession made him frown. She was going to be all over that like a rash. Maybe they should find a nice couch for him to lie on while she took notes. But she didn't say anything, her fingertips moving against his neck in a soothing caress until his shoulders relaxed and he looked into her eyes again. 'If I wanted our first kiss to have an audience, I wouldn't have dragged you over here to dance with me, would I?'

The same understanding he'd seen at the taxi landing entered her eyes. 'You wanted us to be seen together, so everyone knew I was here with you.'

It was uncharacteristically possessive of him—and he didn't know where that had come from either—but he sure as hell wasn't telling her. He'd said enough already.

'We arrived together,' she pointed out with a small smile. 'Wouldn't that kind of make it look like a date?'

They'd met in the foyer, but he got her point.

'It might,' he allowed, 'if you hadn't spent the rest of the night avoiding me and dancing with everyone *but* me.'

'You could have asked me to dance.'

'Sweetheart, I don't stand in line.'

'And I wasn't avoiding you. I was…' She clamped her mouth shut.

'Go on.'

Catching her lower lip between her teeth, she grimaced as it slid free. 'Once I'd introduced you to a few people, I stepped back to let you mingle…and find your feet…'

'Woman, don't baby me.'

She arched a brow. 'Wouldn't sticking to you like glue the entire night be babying you? Kinda like holding your hand while you go play with the big boys?'

Okay. She had him on that one.

'You're an idiot,' she said.

A possessive, jealous idiot, apparently—*that was new.* Not a particularly nice feeling, either.

The hand on his neck slid forward when his gaze scanned the crowd again, and her thumb moved against his cheek. Lifting his arm from her waist, he captured her fingers and lowered them to his chest, his voice low.

'Someone will see you.'

Long, darkened lashes flickered as she lowered her gaze to her hand, her fingers flexing as she took a breath, frowned, damped her lips with the tip of her tongue and looked into his eyes again.

Her hand slid back up. 'I don't care.'

'Yes, you do.'

Capturing her hand, he held it over his heart. 'Forget about it. It's my hang-up, not yours.'

She smiled through another grimace. 'Kinda is mine. I've been so hung up on what people might think if they knew I was sleeping with a client that—'

'Jumping the gun a little bit, don't you think?' He smiled. 'I don't know about you, but I don't like to skip any of the steps. I'm all about the foreplay.'

This earned a burst of soft feminine laughter, and he lowered their hands from his chest, took a step back and threaded their fingers. 'Let's go.'

'Where?'

'Consider it working on your lack of adventure…'

CHAPTER SIX

'*THIS* is a party.'

'Anders!' yelled a chorus of voices over the music.

Olivia was mid-smile when a large palm flattened against the small of her back to guide her through the crowded bar. The heated brand of his touch seared into her skin and scrambled her thoughts. She inhaled sharply.

Those hands should come with a warning.

'Aren't we a little overdressed?' she asked to cover up the effect it had on her.

'One of us is.' He tucked the dark ribbon of his bow tie into the pocket of his jacket, loosened the buttons at the collar of his dress shirt and leaned closer. 'Not that I'm complaining, but I'd have to lose a couple of layers to get to where you are.'

Olivia smiled. The dress was worth every impulsive cent she'd spent on her overextended credit card after she'd left him at the taxi landing.

'Nice monkey suit, Anders.'

'You remember Marty,' Blake said when they got to the table. 'He used to work for me.'

'Still does,' Marty corrected.

'Not if you don't start using my name, you don't.'

'I'm using one of 'em.' He winked at Olivia as he gave up his seat and Blake made the introductions.

'Marty's wife, Chrissy, Sam, Duke, Duke's wife, Kate.' He grinned. 'Happy birthday, beautiful.' She blew him a kiss before he looked at the last person at the table. 'And that's Mitch, but you're better not knowing him—what do you want to drink?'

'We got a pitcher of beer,' Marty offered as he appeared with extra chairs. 'Figure we owe you a drink for the Anders. We're getting a lot of mileage out of that.'

Olivia laughed. 'A beer would be great. Thank you.'

'I'll get another pitcher. Everyone, this is Liv.' Blake's lethal hand moved from her back to her shoulder as she sat down, his thumb rubbing across her collarbone to get her attention. 'Don't believe anything they tell you but feel free to cross-examine them till I get back.'

'What makes you think I'll wait till you're gone?' Before his hand left her shoulder, she turned towards Chrissy. 'So how long did you say you've known him?'

'Since high school.' Chrissy smiled as Blake left. 'It's nice to meet you; we've heard a lot about you.'

They had?

'Marty says you're one heck of a pool player.'

That made more sense. Somehow Blake didn't strike her as the kind of man who discussed the women in his life. Not that she was the woman in his life, but—

Moving on, 'Blake went to high school here?'

'Where didn't he go to high school?' Marty asked as he sat down between them and reached past Olivia for a glass and the pitcher. 'He was here for two semesters when we were seventeen.'

'Made quite an impression on the cheerleading squad,' Chrissy added before smiling affectionately at her husband. 'Well, the *majority* of them, anyway...'

'She already had her eye on a bad boy,' Marty explained

with an equally affectionate smile. 'Been keeping me on the straight and narrow ever since.'

Olivia smiled as she took the glass from him. They were cute together. There weren't many married couples within her social or family circles, but it was easy to tell they were still in love. She wondered how much time Blake spent with them, doubting he would look at them and think of their relationship the same way she did—as something she would like one day, with the right guy, at the right time, given the opportunity.

For a second it made her long for something she could never have with Blake. Someone like him, with a grin that knocked her on her ear, a touch that still tingled on her skin even when he wasn't there, who could make her smile every time she thought of seeing him and who would get jealous when she danced with other men…

She could see herself falling for a guy like that.

'Apart from that time in Canada…'

Olivia perked up. 'Canada?'

'What did I miss?' Blake set another pitcher on the table before removing his jacket and dropping it over the back of the chair beside her.

'We were just getting to the good stuff.'

'They're not going to tell you about Canada,' he said as he rolled up the sleeves of his shirt.

'Canada!' The call came from across the table, glasses raised in salute as the toast was repeated and the men took a drink while the women shook their heads.

Blake chuckled as he sat down. 'Nice try, sweetheart.'

She'd. Been. *That*. Close.

'You know all of them from high school?' she asked when she'd relaxed into a couple of laughter-filled hours.

Leaning closer to hear her over the music, Blake shook his head. 'No.'

The fingertips at the end of the long arm that had been casually resting on the back of her chair traced lazily over the skin of her upper arm. He'd been touching her since he sat down. Apart from the fingertips that hadn't been still for more than a few seconds at a time, she had to deal with his leg brushing against hers, the warmth of his breath close to her ear when he spoke in his rough, rumbling voice and a million other little things that tested the final shred of her resistance.

It wasn't that she hadn't known he had sensational eyes but the thought had never entered her head that the light sparkling in them was probably similar to stars in a night sky away from city lights. It wasn't that she hadn't noticed how thick his eyelashes were or been mesmerized by how sensual each of the sixteen blinks per minute every human being took could be. She just hadn't realised they could hypnotize her to the extent where she felt like staring at him long enough to count the beats in case she missed one...two...three, four...

When his gaze locked on hers, a weird shifting sensation happened inside her chest. Almost immediately, it was replaced with something she recognised: *fear*.

Oh, no. She couldn't allow herself to be sucked in—just because he'd introduced her to his friends and spent the evening treating her like a guy treated a girlfriend didn't mean—she *knew* what she'd been fighting and it had nothing to do with—

'Dance with me.'

'What?' Thankful for the invitation to tear her gaze from his, she glanced at the small dance floor on the other end of the room. 'I don't think—'

'You should do more of that.' He pushed back his chair. 'You overthink things.'

Things like the fact she was the only woman in the

room in a floor-length evening dress and he was asking her to dance to music that leaned more towards hip-hop than tango?

'Don't wimp out on me now, sweetheart.'

Olivia shook her head as she stood up. Glancing at his face, the hint of smugness she detected at how easily he'd played her brought a smile to her face as she stepped past him. He was in so much trouble and he didn't even know it.

Head held high, she ignored the number of people staring at what she was wearing as she made her way through the crowd. Thanks to several strategically placed mirrors in a changing room, she knew what Blake was looking at behind her. The knowledge encouraged her to exaggerate the sway created by walking on sinfully high heels. Judging by the fact a woman at a nearby table slapped her man on the head, she must have been working it to the desired level. A fact she had confirmed when she got to the middle of the dance floor and turned in time to see Blake frown before he lifted his gaze.

Hand on hip, she angled her head and beckoned him to her with a crooked finger. He froze for a second, then closed the gap between them, reached out a hand and raised his voice to be heard over the music.

'I don't think we've met.'

Ignoring the implied suggestion of an introductory handshake, Olivia placed them palm to palm, threaded her fingers through his and lifted their arms as she angled her head a little more and stepped into him.

'We talking or dancing?'

As his head lowered, an arm snaked around her waist. 'We've been dancing since we met.'

Smooth. For a moment she was tempted to smile. But she was the one doing the seducing this time, not him.

Recklessly, she decided he was about to see an Olivia Brannigan few people ever laid eyes on. Gaze lowering to his mouth, she ran her hand up his arm and across a broad shoulder until she could dip her fingers beneath the collar of his shirt and curl them around the column of his neck.

If everyone at the table had been given the impression she was his, in a few moments there wouldn't be a single soul in the entire bar who didn't think every gorgeous inch of him was hers. Fighting her attraction to him was exhausting. Giving in to it—even if it was just for a little while—suddenly seemed much easier.

Leaning forward, she dipped down a little, brushed the tips of her breasts against the wall of his chest and slid upwards, rolling her shoulders and smiling when his body tensed. As they began to sway, she moved her face closer to his, her gaze whispering lazily upwards until she was looking into his eyes. Checking to make sure she had his full and undivided attention, she ran her tongue over her lips, then moved her head so she could speak directly into his ear. 'Did you know dancing is the closest thing to having sex in public?'

'Like living dangerously, do we?'

Pressing tighter to his chest, she allowed her lips to brush his ear. 'I still have the handcuffs…'

'Okay—' he reached for the hand on his neck and took a step back '—*now* we're dancing.'

Tightening long fingers around hers, he took another step back, dropping the hand he'd removed from his neck and swinging her out to arm's length before hauling her back to his chest with a sharp tug. Olivia drew a sharp gasp through her lips as his leg stepped between her thighs; the contact was totally unexpected and at the same time thrilling. The hand on her back tightened, steering her around his body as he changed direction. The leg between her thighs moved back a step, he took another sidestep and, before she knew it, she was being moved around the dance floor.

Did he seriously think she was letting him lead?

When his leg insinuated itself between her thighs again, she stepped higher and back, initiating a back and forth stepping motion that slithered the silky smooth material of her skirt between her thighs with each forward thrust of his leg. But just when she thought she was in control again, he stilled. Clasped hands lifted in the air beside them as he bent her backward, his gaze sliding down her throat to her breasts and back up to linger on her parted lips while he drew her upright and moved his face closer to hers. Heaven help her, it *felt* as if they were having sex in public.

But the woman inside her didn't care, particularly when the pressure of his hand on her lower back brought her abdomen into contact with his groin and she made a discovery. He was as turned on by what they were doing as she was; the evidence pressed against her, heat pooling between her thighs in response. Running her tongue over her teeth, she fixed a heavy-lidded gaze on his mouth as she crushed her breasts against his chest and felt a buzz of anticipation hum through her body.

She was so far over the line she couldn't see it any more but, instead of fear, she felt more alive than she had in years. She'd never cut loose with a man the way she wanted to cut loose with him. Every fantasy she'd ever had, every one of the dreams that left her bathed in sweat and tangled up in her sheets since she met him, she could play out with him. It was too good an opportunity to miss. Call it temporary insanity, a vacation from reality, a reward for all the years she'd spent rebuilding her life and buried in work—she didn't care what her conscience labelled it. She needed this, she wanted him and what was even better, she knew *he* wanted *her.*

Adrenalin pulsed through her veins. Where to begin?

Angling her head, she pushed up onto her toes; a hand gripped his shoulder as she used his large body for leverage until her mouth hovered over his and her inner bad girl looked him straight in the eye.

'Hello, lover.'

Realisation entered his eyes a split second before she hooked her arm around his neck and lifted a foot off the ground. Trusting him to support her weight, she lifted her leg forward and up, curling it over his hip before leaning back and lowering her chin. She looked up at him from beneath her lashes, catching her lower lip between her teeth as she silently transmitted her intentions in the way a man like him would understand.

He shook his head a little. *'Don't do it.'*

If it was meant as a warning, he had a lot to learn about reverse psychology. She slowly slid her thigh down his leg. Back onto her toes and she was sliding upward again. She leaned her head back a little, eyelids heavy and lips parting as she breathed deep and exhaled on a note of sensual satisfaction.

If it felt half as good for him as it did for her…

Gripping her waist with unforgiving fingers, Blake lifted her a couple of inches off the ground, practically throwing her off him before he wrapped his arm around her body and spun them around in circles.

She lifted a brow. 'Something wrong?'

For a moment he looked pained.

'Poor baby,' she pouted, effervescent laughter bubbling inside her chest.

Dark eyes glowed, his gaze glancing briefly over her

head. A faster set of turns made the remaining couples around them clear a space while Olivia's heart beat faster and her blood rushed through her veins. She leaned her head back and closed her eyes, throaty laughter breaking free until he brought them to an abrupt stop, dipped her backward and his large body loomed over hers. With his face shadowed, she focused on his breathing, elated to find it as laboured as hers. She couldn't remember the last time she'd felt so exhilarated, so light and giddy and *free*.

Slowly drawing her upright, he pulled her close again, the curves of her body fitting into the dips and planes of his as if they'd danced together a thousand times. When he stepped back, she stepped forward. There was a give and take to their movements that hadn't been there before, a push and pull all too similar to lovemaking. Now, every time he brushed the inside of her thighs with his leg, she savoured the sensation, moving her leg between his as she followed him forward. When she looked into his eyes, the world went fuzzy around the edges again, her entire focus on him and only him. Did he know how much she wanted him?

How much she *burned* for him?

She wanted the glow in his eyes imprinted on her memory, his touch branded on her skin, his taste in her mouth, to breathe in his scent and have his deep, rough voice echo in her ears. She wasn't stupid—she knew an attraction like theirs didn't come along every day. The fact she knew it would flare and fizzle out didn't matter. If anything, it made it feel as if she had to reach out and grab it before it disappeared and was lost to her for ever.

Her gaze tangled with his as the music changed to something slower. He searched her eyes, studied the loose curl of hair lying against her flushed cheek and watched the movement of her tongue as she damped her lips again. A tremor ran through her at the thought of his mouth against hers, demanding the response she was so ready to give him.

As if he knew how close she was to making their first kiss public, he lifted her hand over her head, turning her around and crossing her arm over her breasts before drawing her back against him and setting his other hand on her stomach, his fingers splayed possessively. While he moved their hips in a languorous circle, Olivia leaned her head back against his shoulder, her eyes closed as his head bowed next to hers. Warm breath tickled against the tingling skin at the hollow of her neck, his body heat seeping through the thin layer of his shirt and into her blood.

She smiled. He was trying to slow things down, wasn't he? It was sweet but there was really no need. Not when she'd made her decision.

She arched her back a little and straightened her legs. The smallest sliding movement, but it had the desired effect. Blake swore beside her ear, the hand on her stomach pressing her tighter to him in an attempt to stop her from doing it again. Swaying her hips in the opposite direction to his in response, she chuckled when the expletive in her ear was more colourful.

Turning around, she reached up, curling the fingers of one hand around his neck while the other framed his face. As his gaze consumed her, she knew, deep down inside where *all* women knew, sex with this man was going to be beyond incredible. One look and her body had begun readying itself for him—had been in pretty much the same state ever since. It was the most basic of biological instincts: the need to mate with the strongest of the species. Was it any wonder she'd been fighting a losing battle when she'd been fighting against nature itself? But she was done fighting. She wanted to feel again. Just for a little while. So long as it was nothing more than physical, she'd be fine.

'Kiss me,' she demanded.

'Here?' The glow in his eyes intensified.

She shook her head. 'Everywhere.'

'I had a more private "here" in mind for that.'

'Then take me home with you.'

He searched her eyes. 'Aren't we skipping some steps?'

'We packed them all into one night.'

'If I take you home with me, we'll be packing a hell of a lot more into one night.' He looked over her head, dark brows folded in thought before he reached for the hand on his face. 'We're leaving.'

A blanket of heated, moist air surrounded them as they left the bar five minutes later, the background noise of traffic and a siren echoing over the river from Manhattan a symphony to her city-girl ears as they rounded a corner and Blake stopped dead in his tracks. Tightening his fingers around hers, he took a deep breath, a muscle working in his jaw before he turned towards her.

'Last chance, Liv. If you've had too much to drink or this isn't something you're one hundred per cent certain you want, I'm not going to be held responsible for the regret you'll have written all over your face tomorrow.'

'You're still an idiot.' She smiled softly, touched by the unexpected chivalry that allowed her a chance to back out. 'I'm not drunk, I know exactly what I'm doing and if you don't shut up and kiss me, I may have to kill you.'

'Why don't *you* kiss *me*?'

'Blake, I *promise you*—'

It was as far as she got before his mouth was on hers. No matter how vivid her imagination had been during waking or sleeping hours, or how real some of those fantasies had felt, nothing could have prepared her for the reality of being kissed by him. Not when hunger and need blinded her to everything but sensation. Firm, warm, practised lips moved over hers, his deliciously clean, masculine scent filling her nose and creating a spinning sensation in her head. He tasted so much better than she'd thought he would—a combination of spice and heat with the tantalising promise of hidden depths if she just pushed a little bit deeper. When he coaxed her lower lip with the tip of his tongue, she opened her mouth and dipped inside.

Shivering when he wrapped his arms around her and drew her to him, the sensation of her overly sensitive breasts crushed hard against the wall of his chest forced her to lift a hand to his shoulder to form a vice-like grip. Leaning into him, she demanded more, the hand at his waist sliding beneath his jacket and tugging at the shirt on his back so she could get to skin.

A groan vibrated in his chest before he tore their mouths apart, leaned his forehead against hers and hauled in a breath, his voice deeper and rougher than before. 'I want to tell you we'll take it slow the first time, but I don't think I can.'

'I just asked you to take me home with you before we'd shared our first kiss—what part of that suggested to you I want to go slow?'

'You know you're going to pay for what you did on that dance floor.'

What did he think she'd been aiming for?

She sighed dramatically. 'And yet somehow we're still standing here, talking about it. Anyone who didn't know you might think you'd been bluffing all this time and you're one of those all talk, no—'

Grabbing her hand in a tight grip, he tugged her to the kerb and whistled loudly. *'Taxi!'*

CHAPTER SEVEN

THE woman slept like the dead.

As the first rays of sunlight appeared in the arched windows of his apartment, Blake watched her sleep. He'd never known anyone who slept so soundly, or remained so still. At least *now* she was still. Several times during the night she'd tested the one chivalrous bone he had left by sliding her naked body against his, smooshing her breasts into his side and rubbing her cheek against his chest. Add the small, contented moaning noises she'd made and his body had spent hours in the same state most men woke up in.

Reaching out, he used the tip of his forefinger to lift a strand of hair from her cheek. She looked exactly the way he'd wanted her to look at the start—hair messed up and framing her face, full lips devoid of lipstick, flushed cheeks... *Damn, they'd been good together...*

She was spectacular when she cut loose. It had been more than worth the effort he'd put into breaking through to get to the woman she kept hidden from the world. *She* was more than worth the effort. Whatever guy ended up spending his life with her would be one lucky—

He frowned. Jealous and possessive—apparently he hadn't shaken either one of them off yet.

His gaze slid down her neck to where the sheet was

dangerously close to slipping off her breast, then lower to where an impossibly long leg was visible, bent at the knee. He remembered how those legs had felt wrapped around him and how responsive she'd been to everything he did and said. It did a lot for a man's ego while at the same time leaving him hungry for more. He wasn't done with her. He was nowhere near done.

Realising he didn't know how long he'd been watching her sleep, he quietly rolled away and eased into a sitting position, scrubbing his fingers haphazardly through his hair. He would let her regain her energy, but he couldn't think of a single reason for her to get out of his bed before Monday.

It took another two hours for her to wake up.

Glancing over his shoulder as she came into the living area, he saw her hands smooth her hair back from her face. She had put on the shirt he had been wearing the night before. The movement of her arms lifted the material up her thighs and he appreciated the fact she'd left several buttons undone at the top, allowing a glimpse of the curve of her breasts.

'There's coffee on the counter,' he said before concentrating on what he was doing, one of his feet propped on the workbench in front of him.

'I can't find my dress.'

'It's hanging up in the bathroom.'

'I borrowed your shirt.'

'I noticed.'

A moment later she appeared at his shoulder with a mug cradled in her hands, her lips pouting as she blew on it before hiding behind the rim.

'Sleep well?'

She nodded as she swallowed. 'Mmm-hmm.'

'Was tempted to check for a pulse a couple of times...'

She didn't comment, but he could feel the change in her; it was as obvious as it would have been if she'd exhaled after holding her breath. He was glad. He didn't want her to regret a single second.

'How long have you lived here?'

'A while.'

'It's nice.' She took another sip of coffee. 'Where did you live before this?'

'Here and there.'

'Always in New York?'

'No.' He took a deep, measured breath. 'But you already know that.'

She'd found him, hadn't she?

When she went for a walk around his living space, he lifted his gaze to the windows in front of him and watched what she was doing. She tilted her head to the side and read the spines of his books and DVDs, lightly ran her fingertips over the back of his sofa, lifted a couple of framed photographs and studied them before setting them down. It was the kind of thing people did in other people's apartments, not that it felt any better.

As she made her way back to him, he lowered his chin and concentrated on the knife in his hand. The blade made a soft, scraping sound as he used his thumb to push it away from his body, carefully guiding each stroke, reducing the wood, layer by layer, to get to what lay beneath. Stopping for a moment, he leaned in and blew on the surface.

Liv stood at his shoulder again. 'Do you think you'll stay here now you have so many apartments to choose from?'

'Chatty first thing in the morning, aren't we?'

'I'm curious.'

'You'll get over it.'

'I don't think so.'

When he looked at her and she smiled a small, soft smile, Blake lowered his foot to the floor. 'Look, Liv, this isn't…'

He frowned. He was going to say it was something he wasn't used to. Given the choice, he avoided the morning after the night before. But he couldn't say that without making it sound as if he slept around or giving her the impression what had happened meant more than it did. Not that it hadn't meant something—*it had*—but he couldn't tell her that either, not without—

'I know,' she said, the smile remaining as she lowered her voice to a conspiratorial whisper. 'Wasn't planning on moving my stuff in for another couple of weeks…'

Blake stared at her as amusement danced in her eyes. Shaking his head, he snagged an arm around her waist and tugged her onto his lap. Nudging her hair back with the tip of his nose, he placed a kiss on the side of her neck before telling her, 'Drink your coffee.'

When she laid an arm across his shoulders and lifted the mug to her mouth, he continued working the wood. For a while there was an almost companionable silence, the blade working as Liv sipped her coffee and watched what he was doing. Whether it was because she'd made it easy for him, or the fact she wasn't walking around looking at his stuff, he didn't know, but whatever it was, it felt better. Even if he realised simply sitting with a woman and enjoying her company was something else that was new.

She looked at some of the finished pieces on the workbench, then down at his hands. 'What's this one going to be?'

'Hasn't told me yet.'

'You don't make it whatever you want it to be?'

'Doesn't work like that.'

She studied his profile. 'How does it work?'

'When you get below the surface, it is what it is.' He lifted the piece of wood and studied it from several angles against the light. 'You either work with that or you toss it away and look for something you like better.'

'What if it's hard to get below the surface?'

'Then you need patience.'

When he looked up at her, sunlight from the window glistened in her hair and her eyes. Lifting a hand to the back of her neck, he eased her towards him, pressing his mouth to her warm, pliant lips. It was a gentler kiss than the majority of the ones they'd shared the night before but, like before, it wasn't enough. Tossing the wood and knife aside, he heard them thud and clatter onto the bench as he wound his fingers around her coffee mug and took it from her hand. Setting it down, he slid his arm under her knees, moved the hand on her neck to her back and pushed to his feet, unceremoniously hoisting her higher.

The vibration of a chuckle against his mouth made him lift his head so he could look down at her. As he smiled in reply, her hand slid from his neck to palm his cheek, her thumb grazing the morning shadow he hadn't dealt with yet.

'I can fix that.'

'No—' she smiled back '—I kinda like it.'

'Remember you said that. I plan on kissing a lot of places I missed last night.'

'I don't think you missed anywhere.'

'Let's check, shall we?'

So long as they stayed the way they were and kept things light, there wasn't any reason they couldn't keep doing what they were doing until he'd finished wrapping things up and went back to his life. Light he could do. Fun he could do. Anything more than that, he didn't have in him. He never had. But as he laid her down on the bed and told her he was going to need his shirt back, for a moment he regretted he was not able to give more. Something else that was new.

She was in love.

'Do not say your two favourite words,' Olivia warned him as they walked across a manicured lawn. 'Not till we're leaving.'

As enthralled as she'd been throughout the thirty-five minute helicopter trip from Manhattan—views of the Empire State Building, Wall Street, the Statue of Liberty, Ellis Island and the Brooklyn Bridge eventually being replaced by open fields brimming with wildflowers, corn, and rows upon rows of sunflowers as they got closer to their destination—she hadn't noticed much as they came in to land beyond glimpses of a large gabled roof surrounded by mature trees. But once they'd walked around the corner of a curving privet hedge and the house was revealed to her in all its glory, she fell instantly and irrevocably in love.

If he dismissed it after his usual five minutes she might have to strangle him. Tearing her gaze from dark shingled walls, white shuttered windows and the curving porch beneath twin turrets, she saw Blake's jaw tense.

'Did you call ahead to say we were coming?'

'I do with all the properties we visit. Why?'

He looked down at her from the corner of his eye. 'Three guesses.'

When she looked for a clue, she discovered a line had formed on the steps at the front door. Stifling a smile, she shrugged. 'At least no one is in a top hat.'

He didn't look amused.

Gravel crunched beneath their feet as Olivia prepared to take on the role she normally did and introduce him. But before she'd opened her mouth, the stately silver-haired man at the head of the line inclined his head.

'Master Blake.'

'We can drop the master part, Henry.'

'Of course, sir…'

Blake shook his head, the next person in line bringing a smile to his face. 'Still here, Martha?'

She beamed in reply. 'It's good to see you again.'

Glancing at the others standing with expectant expressions, he took a deep breath and announced, 'Go home folks—take a few days' paid vacation—we can fend for ourselves.' He winked at Martha on his way past. 'Good to see you, too.'

While she blushed and the rest of the staff looked at each other in confusion, Olivia followed him inside, ignoring her surroundings as she stated the obvious. 'You've been here before.'

'Yes.'

'When?'

'I spent a summer here when I was seventeen.'

Before or after the two semesters he'd spent at high school in Brooklyn? It was a source of great frustration to Olivia that the list of questions she'd formed before she met him grew on a daily basis. After sharing a bed at every available opportunity in the last six days, they knew everything there was to know about each other's bodies but anything more than that, not so much.

Setting her weekend bag and laptop at the bottom of the newel post, she turned towards him. 'You can give me the grand tour, then.'

Blake pressed his mouth into a thin line as he dropped his bag beside hers. 'Fine.'

When he walked through an archway into a room filled with deeply upholstered white sofas, she barely glanced at the understated decor: she was more interested in his reaction to being there.

'Living room.' He waved an arm to his side and kept walking. 'Library.'

She had to increase her pace to keep up.

'Den.' He nodded to the right as they walked back across the hall again. 'Billiard room—that's the British version of pool to you and me—dining room…breakfast room…kitchen…'

'Could we go a bit slower?'

He stopped so abruptly she almost ran into him. 'It's just a house, Liv.'

'The word *just* doesn't come close to describing this place.' She looked up at his face, the realisation hitting her that, 'You don't want to be here.'

Correct her if she was wrong, but hadn't it been his idea? There were plenty of other places they could have visited and they'd barely scratched the surface when it came to the Warren Enterprises' subsidiaries.

Pushing his hands into the pockets of his jeans, Blake turned his profile to her, his gaze fixed on a point outside the numerous windows lining a wall of the large kitchen they were standing in.

He shrugged. 'Thought you'd like it.'

'I do,' she said softly, touched by the comment, even if she didn't entirely believe the trip was solely for her benefit. She smiled when he glanced at her from the corner of his eye. 'I love it. But if you're uncomfortable here…'

'When did I strike you as comfortable in any of the places we've visited?'

Barring the one time, good point, but—

'You want to see outside?'

She noted the swift change of subject, but she nodded, struggling to find patience as he opened a door and they stepped onto an expansive stone patio. Down a couple of sets of gently winding steps and around a corner, a large swimming pool twinkled in the bright sunlight, and the promise of a stunning ocean view from the railing beyond drew them forward. As his large hands grasped the metal railing, Olivia blinked at the horizon and added to her question list. How long had he been here? Had his father spent much time with him? What had it been like? Had they been able to talk? Had his mother been here too? Did they visit regularly?

One question barrelled through the others to make it to the top of the list. 'Why are we here?'

When his fingers tightened, she thought he was not going to answer her. Not that it was anything new, but it was really starting to tick her off.

'I don't know,' he replied in a voice so low she almost didn't hear him.

The fact he was frowning told her he wasn't happy he'd said the words out loud. But what got to her was how much it reminded her of the expression he'd worn on the dance floor when he'd told her he wouldn't hide, *not again*.

'You want the helicopter to come back for us?'

'No.' He let go of the railing and took her hand. 'Let's go look at the best part.'

If it was meant to distract her, it worked, at least for a while. Within five minutes of her toes sinking into warm sand she understood the attraction of The Hamptons. In the city it was easy to become bogged down with a million and one things: deadlines to meet, obligations to fulfil, parties to attend and the vagaries of everyday chores causing stress and tension as people tried to squeeze everything into twenty-four hours per day. It was a hectic, fast-paced lifestyle. One Olivia had thought she thrived on.

But while walking along a deserted beach with her hand

held in Blake's she found herself thinking about the things she was missing out on: the simple pleasures in life it was all too easy to take for granted and the important things she'd relegated to some nebulous point in the future. Her time with him was turning into quite a journey of self-discovery. She smiled wryly. The fact he was so reluctant to talk about his life had made her think about her own.

'It's beautiful here.'

'It is,' he agreed.

Once the silence had been interrupted, she felt the need to fill it. *You could take the girl out of the city...*

'It's funny how easy it is to forget Manhattan is an island. I never think about the ocean being so close. It's just there, you know?' She lifted her hand to push back a strand of hair. 'When I was a kid, we used to take a trip to the beach every summer—Jersey, mostly. My brothers played touch football on the sand, Dad refereed and I got to keep score. Killed me I never got to play. Uneven numbers, they said.'

'How many brothers?'

'Four.'

'Sisters?'

'No, took five attempts for my parents to get it right.' Since she'd opened a line of dialogue, she tried something simple. 'You have brothers or sisters?'

If Charles Warren had more than one child, she assumed they'd have been mentioned in the will, but his mother could have married and had children before or after Blake.

'You're allergic to silence, aren't you?'

'It's called making conversation.'

'We were doing fine without it.'

She stopped and waited for him to turn towards her. 'I can't be the first person to try and get to know you.'

'You're not.'

They hadn't fared any better, had they? Not that it was much consolation.

'You know enough,' he said. 'If you didn't, you wouldn't be sleeping with me.'

Blunt but true. 'You're right, I wouldn't.'

'So what's the problem?'

'Oh, I don't know.' She shrugged. 'Not being made to feel like it could be anyone in your bed would be nice.'

He frowned. 'That's how I make you feel?'

'No.' She searched for a way of explaining what she meant without sounding needy. 'But if you make it seem like I'm not even supposed to make idle conversation with you, I *might* feel that way.'

As she broke eye contact, she shook her head a little, questioning what she was doing. She didn't regret the decision she'd made to sleep with him, no matter how uncharacteristically spur-of-the-moment it may have been. But was it so unusual to want to know even the most basic things about him—the details people shared every day without feeling it had cost them something?

She didn't think so.

'You knew what you were getting into...'

Actually, Olivia wasn't entirely certain she had known, not really. Her attraction to him was an unstoppable force of nature, the conclusion as inevitable as the ocean hitting the shore beside their feet. Beyond that, she may possibly have been a tad naive when it came to how casual she could keep things. Sex was intimate, there was no avoiding that.

'So what is it you want?'

Good question.

'You,' she replied without hesitation.

It was the one thing she was clear on. Her body, still aching with sweet reminders of the passion they shared, though satisfied time and time again, was far from replete. But the needs that weren't being satisfied were beginning to demand similar levels of attention. She wanted to know who she was sharing her body with, to understand how his mind worked, why he reacted to certain things the way he did. The very idea of caring as much as she used to about anything or anyone still terrified her but there had to be a middle ground somewhere.

An affair with a man like Blake could be viewed as a kind of stepping stone—a way of testing the water to discover if she could allow herself to feel again without getting too involved. If it meant being brave and going a little further out on a limb than she'd planned, she could do that—but not at the expense of her self-respect. Jumping into bed with a virtual stranger was one thing, continuing to have sex with him without getting to know him better was another—so yes, she still wanted him but—

'Just not like this.'

'Then why are you here?'

'Because I want to be.' She lifted her chin in defiance, in case he told her she shouldn't feel that way.

'This will end,' he said in the rough-edged rumble that still got to her. 'You know that.'

'I do.'

Blake shook his head, frowning harder. 'Make it more than it is, it'll feel worse when it does.'

She shrugged. 'The memory might be sweeter.'

Turning her head, she looked out at the ocean while retreating behind the wall she'd built around the emotions she could feel churning inside. There may have been a time she'd trusted and was led by her heart, but those days were gone. She couldn't allow herself to get sucked into the maelstrom again but there was a balance to be found, she understood that now. It was something she could take from her time with him.

'Liv—'

'I'm done talking now.' She tilted her head back and took a deep breath of salty air, calmness washing over her as the churning began to settle. 'Just getting it off my chest.' Lowering her chin again, she looked down the long stretch of pale sand in front of them. 'How far does the beach go? Do you want to walk to the end?'

'I'm just supposed to forget what you said?'

She arched a brow at him. 'In case you hadn't noticed, that was me letting you off the hook. I can't afford to get emotionally involved with you, so if that's what you're worried about you can set your mind at ease. Not like there's much point, is there? None of this will matter in a few weeks. Once we've finished scratching this itch—'

The next thing she knew, he was pulling her against him, his mouth capturing hers with brutal intensity. There was nothing gentle in the way he kissed her—nothing tender—but Olivia didn't want gentle or tender. She wanted him to need her as much as she needed him, for him to be even a fraction as out of touch with reality as she felt every time he kissed her. When his fingers splayed across the back of her head and his tongue demanded entrance to her mouth, she opened for him. Their tongues tangled as her hands reached for the strong column of his neck.

Wrenching his mouth from hers, he looked down at her and frowned. He was angry. She could see it. Angry because he'd kissed her, because he hadn't ended it or angry with her for saying what she had? She shook her head. She didn't want to argue with him.

Lifting her mouth, she kissed him with the same urgent sense of need she'd felt when he kissed her. When he groaned and lowered his hands to her hips, she smoothed her hands over his shoulders to his chest, her fingertips exploring the hard, sculpted contours beneath his T-shirt.

'Take me to bed,' she mumbled against his lips.

Their relationship may have been sorely lacking in every other form of communication, but in bed they spoke to each other in ways only lovers could. Having felt the effect even the smallest increase in distance between them could have on her, she needed to feel connected to him again, that he was right there with her, feeling what she felt. It was a Band-aid on what could, if she were foolish enough to let it happen, become a massive gaping wound.

They stopped again and again on the walk back to the house—her shoes dropped inside the kitchen door—his T-shirt gone by the foot of the stairs. When the kissing and tearing at clothes became frantic he leaned back, the twitch of his lips becoming a full-blown grin. Emotion seeped through a crack in the wall around her heart and dripped into her chest.

When had she got so crazy for him?

Fusing their mouths together, he pushed through the door to a bedroom and kicked it shut behind him. But at the side of the bed he stilled, his palms framing her face, thumbs beneath her chin as he looked deep into her eyes.

'You're not just anyone, Liv.' The words were husky and low, washing over her like a caress. 'Don't ever think that. Not when you're with me.'

The impact it had on her heart created fracture lines around the crack, the drip of escaping emotion becoming a trickle. Every danger-sensing instinct she possessed screamed *Run!* but she reached for him, hands smoothing over his chest and around his neck, her voice thick as she demanded, 'Show me.'

Once they were back in Manhattan she would have to think long and hard about what she was doing while she was still in control of her emotions. Even if he had been the kind of guy who stayed in one place, anything more than sex could never be possible between two people unwilling to share more than their bodies. But while he filled her world with warmth, sensation and the physical closeness she'd never experienced with anyone else, she clung to him and held on tight in case she never felt it again.

CHAPTER EIGHT

WATCHING Liv withdraw behind the mask she'd been wearing when he met her had made Blake unreasonably angry. At the same moment she'd made it clear he was hardly in a position to throw stones when it came to communication. It wasn't that he couldn't hold a conversation. Politics, sports, the economy, big business versus the little guy, which superhero would win in a fight with another superhero—he could hold a conversation on a vast range of subjects when he set his mind to it.

It wasn't until Liv that he realised how little he said.

While she slept, he headed outside to clear his head—what had happened on the beach replaying on a loop in his mind while he replaced the things he'd said with what he could have said. When it came to anything about his life, there was a subconscious wall he seemed unable to break through, even though he wanted to—for her.

'Not being made to feel like it could be anyone in your bed would be nice.'

He liked to think he'd taken care of that in the one way he knew he could communicate clearly with her—*anyone, his ass*—but when it came to the other stuff? No, he didn't have any brothers or sisters—had that been so difficult to say? And when he'd asked her what she wanted and her answer had been 'you', why couldn't he tell her it was the same for him? He wouldn't have been telling her anything she didn't already know.

After walking a long loop, he ended up back at the railing overlooking the ocean. When he'd said he hadn't known why they were there, it was the closest he'd come to being open, even if it was only partially true. Maybe he'd thought poking the edge of the empty place inside him with a memory-shaped stick might allow something to leak out; maybe he'd thought he would free an emotion he could experience and deal with before he moved on. If that was what he'd thought, he'd been wrong. He still had a big fat nothing.

Leaning his elbows on the railing, he breathed deep and looked out at the ocean, comparing the seventeen-year-old who'd been there before to the man he was now. He hadn't thought he was as messed up as he'd been back then.

Maybe he'd been wrong.

His gaze followed a seagull as it glided on a current of air, wings outstretched, not a care in the world. Used to be a time he felt that carefree. Thing was, he didn't feel so trapped any more either—as if with each property or asset he disposed of he was cutting a string that attached him to the life he'd never even contemplated. By cutting them he was proving *he* was in control, *he* was the one making decisions, he was in charge of his own destiny. But if that was true, he would be standing at the helm, not feeling as if he were adrift on a raft.

The one time he'd felt like himself had been when he'd looked at the warehouse and thought about its potential. He didn't need penthouses or private jets or skyscrapers with high rental incomes. But building something before he sold it on, something he would only be tied to for the duration of the project, wouldn't be so bad. He could take his usual pride in a job well done while providing steady work for the guys who needed it and had families to think about.

Reaching into the back pocket of his jeans for the envelope, he unfolded it and looked down at the numerous stamps and scored out addresses. It was the first time he'd been tempted to open it.

His chin lifted. Why could he hear music?

Waking up alone wasn't a new experience, but it was starting to get a little annoying when she reached out and he wasn't there. Blinking at the empty space, Olivia resolved it wasn't going to get to her, not when she felt so good. Stretching languorously, arms and legs spread wide in the ridiculously large bed and her head pushed deep into decadent pillows, she grinned from ear to ear. There wasn't an inch of her body that hadn't been worshipped. She curled her toes. A few hours with Blake while he demonstrated she absolutely, most definitely was the woman he wanted in his bed had been *heaven*.

Reluctant to wash his scent from her skin, she got up and threw on light cotton shorts and a halter-neck, padding barefoot through the house and deciding to indulge in a little exploration when she couldn't find him. Starting in the library, she wandered along the floor-to-ceiling bookshelves, trailing her fingertips over the rise and fall of the books' spines as she looked around the room. It would be a great place to spend time on a rainy afternoon. She could see herself taking cushions from the chairs and piling them in the window seat, wrapping a blanket around her legs while she tried to work her way through every book. She'd always meant to find time to read more.

In the fantasy world she allowed herself to envisage for a moment, it was how she would spend her time while Blake was in the workshop he'd set up somewhere in the house. Given the choice, Olivia would make it a bench in the same room—possibly over in the corner where a couple of chairs and a lamp were currently standing—so she could watch what he was doing. The way his hands moved, the concentration on his face as little by little he revealed what was hidden beneath the surface of the wood…

She smiled. She loved watching him work.

In the living room, she stopped to look at pictures of generations of famous Warrens on a baby grand piano, frowning at the fact there weren't any of Blake. He should have been there, laughing and smiling with everyone else. When she found a picture of a young Charles Warren, she picked it up and searched for a resemblance. They had the same colouring, she supposed, but knowing they hadn't been close, she refused to see anything more and set the picture down. He didn't deserve to have his son look like him. Not when he didn't have a single picture of Blake as a baby.

In her fantasy world the few pictures she had seen in his apartment would take up space on the piano along with new ones taken on weekends and holidays at the house. Instead of photographs taken sailing or sipping cocktails or—she leaned in to check what she was seeing, shaking her head in amusement—*playing croquet*, there would be pictures of touch-football on the lawn, picnics on the beach, maybe even snowball fights during winter holidays.

When her imagination started adding kids who looked like Blake to the picture she stopped fantasizing. It was the house calling out to be filled with love and laughter. The more she saw, the deeper she fell under its spell.

In need of something to do, she went to the kitchen and searched through the cupboards for ingredients she could throw together to make a meal that wouldn't require culinary skills or allow her to burn the house to the ground.

With the basics laid out, she placed her hands on her hips and turned a circle. The house had to have a sound system. She'd even settle for a—*Ha!* She might have kept the volume down if there had been houses nearby. But the way Olivia saw it—wherever Blake was—he would soon know she was awake. If she fed him and no one died, they could have an early night.

Leaning his shoulder against the door frame, Blake crossed his ankles and folded his arms across his chest, a smile lifting him out of the contemplative mood he'd been in outside. Unaware of his presence, she balanced salad ingredients in her arms, bumped the refrigerator door shut with her hip and made her way to the sink, where she dropped everything and rescued a pepper as it rolled away.

The singing he'd heard from the patio continued, culminating in an enthusiastic if somewhat off-key chorus of, 'La, la, la…la, la, la… La…la…' as Blake chuckled.

When his gaze followed hers to an overflowing pot, he crossed the room and met her at the stove, the hands he placed on her hips making her jump in surprise before he kissed the side of her neck and she smiled in greeting.

Locating the source of the music, he stepped over and turned the volume down, returning as Liv blew on the surface of a loaded spoon and brought it to his mouth.

His reaction made her grimace. 'That bad?'

It really was. He shook his head. 'No.'

When she sighed heavily, he took the spoon out of her hand, turned her around and moved her to the side before lifting her and setting her on the counter. 'Do I want to know what's in the other pot?'

'Pasta.'

'How long have you been boiling it?'

'Ten, fifteen minutes.' She shrugged.

'I'd say it's done then, wouldn't you?'

'I don't spend much time in the kitchen.'

'I guessed.'

Turning off the heat, he set the pans to the back of the stove. 'How have you managed to survive this long without learning to cook?'

'I live in Manhattan, I don't need to cook. We have delis and restaurants and markets where you can buy stuff that's already put together in neat little packages you can heat up in the microwave.'

'If Martha had more notice we were coming you'd have found something similar in the refrigerator.' Checking what she'd left by the sink, he set the things he needed aside and started opening cupboards. 'Last time I was here, she made enough food for an army.'

When he looked at her again Liv had a thoughtful expression on her face. Considering his reaction when she asked questions, he could understand that but he didn't mind talking about Martha. She was one of the few good memories he had from that summer. The kitchen had been different then: a large wooden table in the centre of the room had provided the setting for the three squares a day. A younger, cockier Blake had flirted outrageously with the older woman because he knew it made her blush.

'You want something to drink?' he asked.

'What is there?'

'In this place—name your poison.'

'I'll have what you're having.'

After a trip to the refrigerator, he opened drawers until he found utensils, popping the lids off ice cold bottles of beer and handing her one before he washed his hands at the sink and got to work.

Taking a sip from her bottle, Liv ran the tip of her tongue over her lips. 'Did Martha teach you to cook?'

Lowering his chin, he focused on chopping the pepper into strips, the knife making efficient, even slices. 'No one but Martha cooks in this kitchen when Martha's here.' He took a short breath. 'My mom taught me the basics.'

Giving her an opening hadn't cost him much. It was dealing with the line of questioning she could form from it he wouldn't find easy. Thanks to his upbringing, he had a tendency to think three steps ahead. Don't say anything that might give people a hint where he came from or where he was going. Never mention something that would lead to another question and another until they had enough pieces to put it all together. When he'd said he wouldn't hide, he'd meant it, but the truth was he'd been conditioned to hide. Probably half his problem, now he thought about it.

'Mine tried that,' she replied lightly. 'Still does from time to time. Not that it does her much good.'

He smiled. 'Tomboy, huh?'

'Didn't matter, she tried it with all of us. No division of the sexes in the Brannigan household.'

'Four brothers can't have made your life easy.'

'You have *no idea.*'

No, he didn't. But he was glad about that for many reasons, not least of them being he hadn't had anyone to worry about but himself.

'Were you serious about your brother running a background check on every guy he sees you with?'

'They all do.'

Blake's brows lifted. 'They're all cops?'

'Worried they might find something?'

'No.' He smiled again. 'Are you?'

'You're not on the Mounties' Most Wanted list?'

His smile grew. 'Killing you to know what happened in Canada, isn't it?'

'Yes.'

'Can't tell you, sweetheart; I took an oath.'

'Attorney/client confidentiality, remember?'

'Pity you're off the clock then, isn't it?'

'Damn it.' She was silent for a moment, the sparkling memory of an earlier time in their relationship fading in her eyes before she felt the need to add, 'You know I'm not billing you for the hours we're together like this, right?'

'You have to bill me for today and tomorrow. Weekend starts Saturday.'

'Changes my profession a tad, don't you think?'

'You're here because we're looking at another property.' He slanted a glance at her to measure her reaction. 'If you don't bill me, they're more likely to question what you've been doing.'

She thought about that. 'It just doesn't feel right. And anyway—' she shrugged the shoulder nearest to him '—I'm hardly the first person in the world to play hooky, am I?'

'You've never played hooky before,' he said with the certainty of someone who had played it plenty.

'There's a first time for everything.' She smiled, her gaze rolling upward. 'Been kinda fun...'

He was glad to hear it but, 'Bill me for office hours, Liv. Keep it straight with your boss.'

'Not when we're doing...*this*...' she said with a wave of her hand between them.

'We've been doing *this* since the day we met.'

'Not all of it, we haven't.'

'So where do you suggest we draw the line?'

'I don't know,' she said honestly. 'But we'll figure it out.'

'It's not like I can't afford it.'

She could quadruple her rate as far as he was concerned. People with money tended to pay over the odds for the best and, whether he liked it or not, he was now one of those people. Since he'd watched her at work she could consider half of it a bonus for how sexy it was when she talked in legal terms. The way she said 'fiduciary' did it for him every damn time.

'That's not the point.' She sighed.

Setting the knife down, he rinsed his hands again and picked up a cloth to dry them. 'No one knows you're sleeping with me, if that's what you're worried about. It's not like we're having sex in Times Square.'

She frowned. 'Are we heading for an argument? I don't know about you, but I'd prefer it if that didn't happen.'

'There's nothing to argue about. You bill me for office hours, we'll take it from there.'

'No,' she said firmly. 'And I'm not moving on that. Not while we're here.'

Tossing the cloth, he turned towards her. 'So you're gonna do what when we're not here? Check your watch every time I kiss you, or are you going to make a rough estimate of how much time we spend flirting and deduct it from the weekly total?'

'Don't do that,' she warned. 'You're making this more complicated than it needs to be.'

'No, what I'm doing is making it *less* complicated.'

Shaking her head, she set her bottle down and began to wriggle off the counter. 'You're the most stubborn person I've ever met.'

'I'm not holding all the cards on that one.' Stepping sideways, he laid his palms flat on the counter beside her hips and looked deep into her eyes. 'You think I want you doing math in your head when you're with me?'

'That's the whole point of not billing you while we're here,' she said with exasperation. 'I want our time here to be about this...about *us*...'

When she realised what she'd said she frowned, her gaze lowering to his neck. But before he could tell her not to censor herself, her chin lifted, eyes bright with determination as if looking at him as she said the words was some kind of personal challenge. 'Can you give me that?'

Blake was floored by how much he wanted to. In that moment, looking into her eyes, he wanted to give her everything. Anything she wanted was hers; all she had to do was ask. It was the first time having stupid amounts of money held any appeal to him. He couldn't promise her more than he was already giving her from a personal point of view, not when he didn't think he had it in him. But this time in this place he could give her, even if it still didn't feel like enough.

Hands moving from the counter to her hips, he nodded.

The smile she gave him was different from any of the smiles he'd seen before. 'Told you we'd figure it out.'

Reaching up, she palmed his cheek before leaning in and kissing him. Her soft lips explored his as she lifted her legs and wrapped them around his thighs to haul him closer. Hands sliding up from her hips, Blake circled her waist and drew her to him, angling his head to deepen the kiss.

'Thought you were hungry,' he mumbled.

'I am,' she mumbled back. 'But not for food.'

'Think you can stay awake long enough to eat later?'

Liv leaned back and blinked as he slid her off the counter. 'Are you complaining because we don't snuggle? Oh. That's. So. *Sweet.*'

Shaking his head, he allowed her feet to hit the floor before scooping her into his arms and turning around. 'You sleep like a dead person.'

'It's not my fault you tire me out.'

'I happen to *enjoy* tiring you out.'

'I'm obviously not doing as good a job of it with you.' She nodded firmly. 'I'll try harder this time.'

Heaven help him if she did.

She smiled the smile he hadn't pinned down yet. 'Would be nice—just once—to wake up and find you beside me.'

It was something else he could give her.

CHAPTER NINE

'YOU want more coffee?'

'Please.'

Raising a hand to the back of her neck, Olivia moved her fingers against tense muscles. Sitting at a table for three hours without a break would have made her muscles ache to begin with but working with Blake wasn't helping any. She'd never been so distracted from her work by the presence of another human being. Every movement of his large hands, the rise and fall of his broad chest beneath the dark material of his V-necked T-shirt, the teasing hints of deliciously clean male scent that drifted across to her when he shifted his weight in his chair or—

It was distracting as hell.

Lifting the mug he set in front of her, she cradled it in both hands and leaned back in her chair, blowing on the surface of the hot liquid before she took a sip. When her gaze found his, he was watching her mouth.

'You could just let it sit till it cooled.'

She shrugged. 'Maybe I needed the break.'

'This was your idea.'

True—kind of made a mockery of their time there being about 'us'—but she saw it as a necessary survival tactic. Her hope might have been they'd get to know each other well enough to make it feel as if what they were doing was more than just sex for its own sake—that it could be categorised as a romantic interlude when she looked back on it in her old age. But who could have predicted after a minor breakthrough in the conversation department that the first real change would take place in the bedroom? After endless hours of couldn't-keep-their-hands-off-each-other sex, if she'd known the difference it would make when he made love to her oh-so-slow with soul-shattering tenderness—looking deep into her eyes as she tumbled over the precipice…

Trouble was, she wasn't convinced she'd have done anything different. But the experience had widened the crack around her heart, turning the trickle of escaping emotion into a flow she was fearful she wouldn't be able to stem if it got any worse.

'How many shares does this guy have?' He lifted the paper he'd been reading and turned it towards her so she could see the details.

Reaching out a hand, she called up the information. 'Ten per cent.'

'This one?'

'Six per cent.'

'So Kirby is the largest shareholder on the board…'

'No. *You're* the largest shareholder on the board.' Having decided his lack of interest in money was yet another thing she found sexy, she transferred her attention to how tiny the pen looked in his hand.

'Collectively, they could still outvote me.'

'They're only going to outvote you on something they don't think will make money. That's the way it works when you're a shareholder.'

'Thanks for the heads-up,' he said dryly.

Her gaze lifted. 'I'm just stating a fact.'

'Do I have the word *stupid* written on my forehead?'

'No. But I'm pretty sure I can see the word *touchy*.' She sighed. 'If you hate this so much, wouldn't it be easier to sell your shares with everything else?'

His eyes narrowed. 'You don't approve.'

'Do you need my approval?'

'No.'

'Then why should my opinion matter?' She smiled sweetly. 'If I recall, I'm not supposed to have one.'

Leaning back in the chair, he rolled his neck before tossing his pen on the table. 'I'm done for today.'

'Do you want to tell me what the problem is or shall I take a stab at it?'

'Not a big fan of paperwork.'

'Mmm-hmm—' she nodded '—got that.'

When she continued staring at him, he frowned. 'Might save time if you told me what you're fishing for...'

'Admitting you don't want to take over the day-to-day running of the company might be a good place to start.'

'I don't want to take over the day-to-day running of the company.'

'Because you don't want to or because you don't think you can?'

Blake nodded, pressing his mouth into a thin line. 'I'd stop there if I were you.'

'No, you wouldn't.'

He turned his head and looked out of the windows. 'I don't want the responsibility.'

'Okay.'

He shot her a warning glance from the corner of his eye. 'Don't play me, Liv.'

'Touchy.' She shook her head. 'You're still not easy to work with, you know.' When he lifted a brow, she rolled her eyes. 'Fine. *Work for*.'

A tense silence descended. One she didn't fill for a

minute. Deciding that was ample demonstration of patience—and since talking about work was a safe subject—she set her mug down and rested her elbows on the table. 'Walk me through it. Which part of the responsibility is it that bothers you most?'

He looked into her eyes. 'You won't change my mind.'

'What makes you think I want to?'

'Don't you?'

'Depends how dumb I think your reasoning is…'

'I made it clear from the start how I felt about all this.' He shook his head again. 'Not everyone wants to live the billionaire CEO lifestyle.'

'I think you'll find the majority of people would be willing to try the billionaire part.' She took a short breath. 'Even if you sell everything at knock-down, everything-must-go prices, you're still going to end up with buckets of money. What are you going to do then—let it sit and gain interest? 'Cos it will, you know. Money makes money. It's like bacteria in a Petri dish.'

'Maybe I'm considering giving it away,' he said with a completely straight face.

Olivia's eyes widened in disbelief. 'You're just going to hand it out on street corners? Do you have any idea how long that would take?'

'I could hire you to do it.'

She laughed. 'Sorry to disappoint, but I wasn't planning on making a lifetime commitment to you.'

The comment earned another frown. 'I don't expect you to understand.'

It was getting tough to keep the note of exasperation from her voice. 'Have you considered the difference it could make to your life? You could do what you want when you want.'

'I already do.'

'You could make a difference with this money.'

'Giving it to people who need it wouldn't do that?'

It wasn't that he didn't have the right to do whatever he wanted with his legacy. Of course he did. It was just Olivia didn't get it and since it was wrapped up in her need to understand how his mind worked...

'Thousands of people work for Warren Enterprises.'

He folded his arms. 'I remember the guilt card from the first time you played it.'

'There might be more jobs if you ran the place.'

'Still might. Doesn't mean I have to be there. Didn't you say there are people at the company who know what they're doing?'

Oh, he was *good*. She'd argued with trial attorneys who weren't half as quick-minded as he was.

'There's nothing you want to keep from all this?'

Suspicion narrowed his eyes. 'Like?'

Her gaze slanted briefly to the side. 'Nothing you want to hang on to...'

'I might need a bigger hint.'

'No *properties* that interest you?'

'It's just a house, Liv.'

'Don't listen, baby,' she crooned to the house before aiming a glare at him. 'You can fall for a crappy, rundown warehouse but can't envisage wanting to spend time in this beautiful place? Have you had your eyes tested recently?'

'There's nothing wrong with my eyes.'

Actually, she would have to agree with that. She loved his eyes. She just wished she could read what was going on behind them a bit better.

'The warehouse is different,' he said.

'Different how—apart from the obvious falling apart versus still standing aspect of it all...?'

'I can see the potential in it.' Unfolding his arms, he reached for his mug. 'Maybe he knew that.'

It was said as if he found it difficult to believe even his father knew him that well. Tilting her head, Olivia studied him while she tried to slot the information into place. There was a danger it would take them out of safe topic for conversation territory, but if he thought she was giving up on the house she loved so much…

'You can't see potential in this place?' She tried a tentative, 'Because it has memories?'

'It does.' He nodded.

Not good, she assumed. 'You could make new ones.'

'What makes you think we haven't done that already?'

The need to smile was immediate, the flow of emotion escaping into her chest increasing. But when the intensity of his gaze made it feel as if he could see inside her, she leaned back, frowned and pushed to her feet. Walking around the table, she circled his wrist with her fingers, took the coffee mug, set it down and reached for his hands. 'Come on.'

'Where are we going?'

Releasing one hand, she led him down the hall by the other. 'You'll see.'

In the middle of the library, he lifted his brows in question. 'What am I looking at?'

'It's called a library. The books should be a clue for you.' She stepped to his side, tilting her head as she looked up at him. 'What would you change?'

'No point changing anything if I'm not keeping it.'

'What about the bookshelves?' She looked at the room. 'Would you change them?'

'If they're holding up books, I'd say they're doing their job.'

Leaning closer, she adopted a tone of mild outrage. 'But they painted over all that lovely wood.'

'Not all wood is lovely. They probably painted over it for a reason.'

'When money isn't a problem?'

He shook his head. 'You want to strip the paint off that many shelves, it would be quicker ripping them out and starting again.'

Olivia frowned at the idea, suddenly protective of the room. 'Is that what you'd do?'

'I'd leave them the way they are.' He leaned down and lowered his voice. *'Less work.'*

'So there's *nothing* in here you'd change.'

'Since you've obviously put some thought into it, why don't you tell me what *you'd* change?'

'It's not mine to change,' she replied in an echo of the conversation they'd had at the plaza.

'If it was...'

'W-ell...' she scrunched her nose a little as she fought the impulse for all of two seconds before enthusiasm slipped free '...okay, then.' Releasing his hand, she stepped forward with a spring in her step. 'Nice deep cushions in the window seats—there's too much white in here, so I'd change the drapes. You know—add a little warmth to the colour scheme...'

'That's cosmetic. You're not changing the room.'

'I *like* the room,' she said as she turned towards him and shrugged a shoulder. 'It just feels like there's something missing.'

'Coving,' he said without missing a beat.

'What?'

'Some genius took out the coving.' She tilted her head back and studied the high ceiling. 'Would it be hard to put it back in?'

'No. But finding it might take time. You want to replace like-with-like where you can in a place like this.'

Lowering her chin, she studied his face, trying to figure out if he was talking the way he would if he was consulting instead of making decisions about a place he could call his own. 'So that's what you'd do? You'd hunt around salvage yards or antique stores until you found it?'

Not that she had any idea where people got stuff like that, but she assumed it was one or the other.

'I know a guy. I tell him what I need, he tracks it down.' He shrugged. 'What I can't find, I make. It's because I can reproduce traditional carving people hire me for renovations of old buildings.'

'So you'd do the work yourself.' Olivia smiled.

'Why would I hire someone to do something I can do?'

'And *enjoy* doing.'

'Fine.' Blake shook his head in resignation. 'I'd replace the fronts of the shelves.'

Her smile grew. 'With something carved?'

'Rope, maybe shells, something nautical to reflect the fact the ocean is outside.'

Clasping one large hand in two of hers, she backed away. 'Next room.'

'You've made your point,' he said as he allowed her to lead him across the hall.

'I'm just getting started.'

Stopping inside the doorway, she lifted her brows.

'Billiard room,' he supplied with a hint of amusement in his eyes. 'The big green table gave it away.'

'Do you play billiards?'

'No.'

'You play *pool*.'

'I'd take the billiard table out and replace it with a pool

table.' He shook his head again, the amusement more obvious. 'That's what you want me to say, right?'

'Would leave a lot more space…'

'A whole two feet of it…'

'Wouldn't have to be smack bang in the middle, the way this one is, though. It's a big room.'

'Be a pain in the ass to get out of here.' When he looked at her again and she batted her eyelashes in reply, she was rewarded with a smile. 'And you had time to think about all this when, exactly?'

'That was a pretty long walk you took yesterday.'

'It wasn't *that* long.'

'Yes, it was.'

'Missed me, did you?'

'You want to know what I think could go in here?'

'Go on.'

She pointed to a corner. 'Big-screen TV over there for watching the games. Big leather sofa in front of it. Maybe a bar over here—you could carve something beautiful like the bed you were working on that day…'

'Was that a compliment?' He chuckled when she rolled her eyes. 'If we're putting in a bar, we need a jukebox.'

'Not one of those new ones.' She frowned.

'Rock 'n' roll era—we could put a pinball machine beside it.'

'See?' She beamed. 'Now you're getting it.'

'We're not doing this for every room,' he said firmly.

'Well, duh, we can't have a pool table in every room. Where would our friends sit when they come to visit?' When she realised she'd stepped into fantasy land, she blinked and tugged on his hand. 'Just a couple more rooms.'

It went pretty well in the den, Blake playing along with less reluctance as they decided the furniture could be moved and it was the perfect room to sit around an open fire in winter. It was the announcement of 'one more room, I swear'—the step too far she just *had* to take—that messed it up.

Having only seen it from the hall, she wasn't overly surprised when he lingered in the doorway, allowing her hand to slip from his as she walked further into the room.

'I know,' she said as she sat down at a huge leather-topped desk and swivelled the chair around to face him. 'Kind of oppressive, isn't it?'

Blake's gaze roved over the wood panelled walls as he leaned against the door frame and pushed his hands into his pockets. 'I used to think so.'

The hollow tone sounded a death knell on her plan to let him see the potential for a home in the house she loved so much. Olivia grimaced. 'This is his office.'

'Was.' He looked around again. 'Probably inherited—panelling looks original.'

'It's dark,' she commented cautiously.

'Dark wood to begin with but wood does that over time. Strip the varnish, it would probably look better.'

When his gaze found hers, Olivia's chest deflated. One step forward, three steps back. She didn't know to quit when she was ahead.

'I didn't think. I'm sorry.'

'It's just another room, Liv.'

If it was just another room then the hollow tone of his voice wouldn't make it feel as if everything should be taken out and burned so there was nothing left of Charles Warren. What kind of father didn't try to have a relationship with his son? How could that man have walked around in the guise of a well respected businessman and philanthropist while behind closed doors he didn't have so much as *one photograph*—?

Laying her hands flat on the desk to push the chair back, her gaze fell on one of numerous picture frames on the surface. Frowning, she lifted one as she stood up.

'This is you.' Her gaze slid over the others. 'They're all of you.'

It was his childhood in a patchwork quilt of different sizes and styles of frames. To Olivia, it felt as if she'd discovered El Dorado. He just would have been an adorable baby, wouldn't he? How could anyone have resisted that smile? She bit the corner of her lip when she spotted a later picture.

'Nice hairstyle.' Setting down one frame, she reached for another. 'I take it back.'

'Take what back?'

'What I thought last night.' She pointed the frame in her hand in the general direction of the living room. 'There are a bunch of family photos in the other room.'

'And?'

'There weren't any of you.' she shrugged a shoulder as she set the frame down. 'I thought there should be—blamed him because there weren't—but now I know he had *these…*'

Reaching for a picture taken at the railing by the pool, she frowned at the awkwardness between father and son. There was a visible gap between them, Blake's body language suggesting he was less than happy about having his picture taken. Not unusual for a teenager, but she sensed there was more to it than that.

She shook her head. 'I don't get it. Why aren't there any out there? Did he spend that much time in here?'

Gaze lifting sharply when she realised she'd asked the questions out loud, she searched Blake's face for a sign she'd overstepped. He frowned, his gaze on the backs of the pictures not visible from the doorway as a muscle worked in his jaw.

'He couldn't put them with the others.'

Her brows lifted. 'In case someone *saw them*?'

When he nodded, any feelings of forgiveness she'd had disappeared with the snap of invisible fingers. *'Why?'*

It explained why no one had heard of him. Why he was such a mystery when his name appeared in the will and why it had taken so long to find him. But at the same time it made her ache. She could see his face as he'd said he wouldn't hide, *not again.* To purposely hide a child from the world, denying his existence until he was forced into the open as an adult and pushed into a life he hadn't wanted to live, it was so…*manipulative*… What was worse, she'd been part of it. She'd thought he was insane to turn it down, had been determined he should accept the responsibility of such a 'great' legacy.

Olivia felt nauseous.

'He wasn't allowed.'

'What do you mean, he wasn't allowed?' A hint of barely suppressed anger threaded her voice. She wasn't buying it. There was virtually nothing a man with Charles Warren's wealth and power couldn't do if he *wanted to.*

'He made a deal,' he replied in the same hollow tone.

'What kind of deal?'

'She didn't give him a choice.'

Meaning his *mother*? While frantically attempting to make sense of it all, she tried to work out what it was she could see behind dull, emotionless eyes. Resignation, acceptance—what was it? When it occurred to her what it *might be*, it hit her with the equivalent force of being run over by a speeding truck. It wasn't something she could see; it was something she thought she could sense because she knew how it felt.

Standing in the doorway, so tall, still and in control, one of the strongest-willed men she'd ever met suddenly seemed *vulnerable*. And. It. Killed. Her.

Blake's eyes narrowed almost imperceptibly, his jaw tight as he spoke through clenched teeth. 'Don't do that.'

Oh, yeah, *now* he was angry. But not at his parents, not at the past—he was angry at *her*.

When he pushed off the doorway and disappeared into the hall, something inside her snapped. She wanted to *know him*. Not be made to feel as if she were being locked out of his thoughts and how he felt because she didn't matter. Why make the effort to demonstrate so definitively she wasn't just any woman in his bed if how she felt didn't matter? She'd tried not to get emotionally involved but she couldn't change who she was—not that much. It had been there all along. The churning emotion she'd held so tightly in check constantly bubbled below the surface, waiting for a crack in the shell around her heart to grow wide enough for some of it to escape.

Wavering, she made a vain last-ditch attempt to force it back inside and give the moment of madness an opportunity to pass. But it was too late. She cared about him and in six years' time she didn't want to be haunted by what had happened between them.

'She couldn't walk away with dozens of unanswered questions and 'what ifs'…

Not again.

CHAPTER TEN

'YOU can't just drop something like that on me and walk away,' Liv's voice said behind him.

Gaze fixed on the door at the end of the hall, Blake sensed the freedom beyond, drawn to it with the same compulsion that made a man kick to get to the surface of deep water so he could haul in air. It was an urge he recognised, the restlessness inside him as ingrained as the screaming instincts he'd ignored when he told her things she didn't need to know.

'Damn it, Blake.' Frustration threaded her voice. 'Would you just stand still for a minute?'

Yeah, he was famous for standing still, wasn't he? Thing was, for a moment, while they'd been talking about changes that could be made to the house, he'd thought—

'Talk to me.'

So she could land another dose of pity on him? He didn't think so. Close to the door, he changed direction, reasoning if he was going anywhere, he needed his stuff.

'Of course, how stupid of me,' her voice said when he was halfway up the stairs. 'This is what you do. It's why you've had so many addresses. You run away.'

Hands clenched into fists at his sides, he froze and fought the wave of anger washing over him. 'You don't know anything about me.'

'Why do you think I'm trying to get to know you?'

Breathing deep, he took another upward step.

'Going to pack, are we?'

It was none of her damn business what he did or where he went. There was a difference between running away and leaving somewhere he just plain didn't want to be.

'That's your life, is it? Every time someone tries to get to know you, you cut and run.' She laughed bitterly. 'So much for not hiding.'

Anything you say can and will be used against you.

Squaring his shoulders, he turned around. 'When did pushing me start to seem like a good idea to you?'

'Being patient wasn't getting me anywhere, was it?' Anger flashed in her eyes. 'You think I like sleeping with a stranger?'

'Seems to me you liked it plenty last night.' He bit back the way any animal would when backed into a corner.

'Seems to me I wasn't *alone* last night.' She lifted her chin in defiance. 'See, that's what I don't get. The stranger I sleep with? He's a pretty amazing guy. That's why I'd like to get to know him better. The man I spend time with during the day—most of the time he's not bad—but he could win Jerk of the Year with very little effort.'

Blake pressed his mouth into a thin line. If she wanted to get it off her chest he could be the big guy and take it, but once she'd spit it all out they'd be done.

She lifted a hand and dropped it to her side. 'What do you think I'm going to do? Try and pin you down to a long-term commitment? Start planning a wedding and naming our kids the second you tell me something about your life? When did I strike you as someone desperately looking for a happily ever after? If I was, I sure as hell wouldn't be looking at you.'

That really shouldn't have bugged him as much as it did. 'Maybe you should tell me what it is you *do* want.'

'I want you. To. Talk. To. Me.'

'So we can work our way through my childhood issues?' He jerked his brows. 'I didn't realise therapist training was part of the course at law school.'

'You think you're the only person who has been messed up by something that happened in the past?' she yelled.

Blake laughed and shook his head. 'You're so far over the line of good judgement now you're flailing.' He looked her straight in the eye. 'You know *squat* about being messed up or what it takes to walk out the other side of it.'

'You think?'

'I know.'

Glancing down the hall, she nodded, eyes glinting with raw emotion when she looked at him again. 'When you've spent six years of your life believing if you'd just done one thing different you might have saved someone's life then you can talk to me about being messed up and what it takes to come out the other side of it. Okay?' She took a breath, shook her head and turned on her heel, her voice cold and controlled. 'I'm done. Talk to me, don't talk to me. Do whatever the hell you want. At least I'll know I tried.'

Blake ground his teeth together, determined he was going to let it go. Just because every time she took a step back he felt the need to take a step forward didn't mean—

'I can't.'

She was on the other side of the banister from him when the words slipped out, surprising him as much as her. Blinking, he shook his head as she stopped and looked at him. What the hell was he doing?

'Yes, you can,' she said in a low voice.

'No.' It took more effort to say it again. 'I *can't.*'

The emphasis made her pause before asking, 'Why not?'

'It's not something I do.'

'You could try.'

'It's not that simple.'

Great, now he couldn't keep his damn mouth *shut*. He tried to figure out why he was still there. Didn't want to leave was the obvious answer. Understanding the underlying cause was a different matter. Since there was only one way he could find out, he sat down on the stairs, setting his feet apart and leaning his elbows on his knees before he looked at her through the carved wooden balustrade.

'I'm not big on sharing.'

'Because it's not easy for you,' she said tentatively.

'Because I'm not any good at it.' He frowned.

Avoiding his gaze, she took a short breath, narrowed her eyes and pointed a finger at him. *'Stay there.'*

Climbing the stairs, she sat down a couple of steps below him, her back to the wall as she waited for him to decide what to tell her.

'I can hold a conversation,' he heard his traitorous voice explain. 'I just can't…'

Form a sentence, apparently.

'It's okay, I get it now.'

Good. Maybe she could explain it to him.

'You didn't get it five minutes ago.'

'That was different.' She shrugged when he looked at her. 'I didn't know why, then.'

And that was all it took to appease her?

'Makes sense…'

It did?

'Easier to tell when someone is holding stuff back if it's something you do yourself. You've always known when I was doing it, even when I thought I had my game face on.' She grimaced. 'I don't find this easy, either.'

'Not like I make it easy for you.'

She rolled her eyes. 'Shocking as it is to believe, it's not actually all about you.'

Okay, he'd deserved that.

She smiled a small smile. 'Has there ever been a time you spit something out without thinking about it first?'

A corner of his mouth tugged wryly. She had to ask?

'I mean personal stuff.'

'No.'

'You're like that with everyone?'

'Yes.'

'What about Marty—you guys seemed pretty tight.'

'We talk the way guys talk.'

'Sports analogies, right?' Her eyes sparkled. 'I can talk in football terms if it helps.'

Blake lifted his brows. 'Know what *would* help?'

'Not patronizing you?'

She'd got it in one. When she studied him again, he waited.

'I can't believe I'm going to say this.' She sighed heavily. 'Tell me what you're thinking.'

'You know the problem with that?'

'Apart from the fact it's lame?'

He let her in on a little secret. 'When women ask that question, whatever a guy was thinking is replaced with what he *thinks* he should be thinking.'

'Is that what you do?' She blinked innocently.

'I tend to ignore the question.'

When the smile softened her eyes, Blake shook his head. Fighting the need to close some of the distance between them for all of ten seconds, he reached for her hand, spreading his legs wider to make enough room to tug her onto the step below him. As she leaned back against his chest, he pressed the tip of his nose to soft summer-scented hair and breathed deep, allowing her body heat to seep into him before he rested his chin on her head and frowned at the tremor he could feel running through her.

Gently rocking their bodies, he waited until he felt her take several long, controlled breaths before the shaking eased and she relaxed into him.

'Right now,' he said in a low voice as he lifted his head, 'I'm thinking I'd really like to know what happened six years ago but I can't ask you to tell me.'

'Why?'

'Bit hypocritical, don't you think?' He looked down at her as she rested her head against his shoulder. 'You share stuff with me, you'll expect it in return.'

'Sharing does tend to involve more than one person.'

'You've got the wrong guy for that.'

'Do you want to try?'

'I can't change the past, Liv. Talking about it isn't going to undo anything.' As he said the words he felt the emptiness inside him grow.

'Shall I tell you what I think?'

She was asking for permission?

'I think we have the perfect scenario for sharing stuff. We're those passing ships in the night. But I don't think it matters if you know someone for five minutes or fifty years, they all become part of your journey if you let them.' The smile sounded in her voice. 'I know that probably sounds dumb to you, but—'

'No, it doesn't. I've met people like that.'

She looked up at him. 'Name one.'

'Matthew Allen. Taught me to carve wood.' He smiled at the memory. 'Grumpy old bastard, but he had tales to tell. He could see things in a lump of wood anyone else would have burnt. Left me his tools when he died…'

A legacy he'd appreciated from a man who had been

more of a father to him in six months than Charlie Warren had been in a lifetime. He'd mourned Matthew's passing. He could access what he'd felt at the time with very little effort.

'And now I know something I didn't know before…'

Nodding, Blake considered what she'd said and thought about the raw emotion he'd seen in her eyes when she'd revealed more than she intended to in the heat of the moment. He liked the idea of being part of her journey—leaving the same indelible imprint on her it felt as if she was leaving on him. What he didn't want was the time they spent together to be seen as a mistake or for it to hurt when she thought about it in the future.

How she felt mattered to him. It may have crept up on him when he'd been distracted by everything else but it had been there for a while.

'If I'm going to try this, you can't look at me the way you did in that room.'

'How did I look at you?'

'Like a kicked puppy.' He frowned. 'I don't need your pity, sweetheart.'

'You thought that was pity?' She looked stunned.

'What was it, then?'

'I can tell you it wasn't pity.' She shook her head. 'The problem with only getting pieces of the puzzle is people have a tendency to fill in the gaps. I went from resenting your father to forgiving him a little to hating him and angry as hell in less than ten minutes.'

Blake was tempted to welcome her to his seventeen-year-old world.

Lowering her chin, she watched as she smoothed her palm over his arm in a light caress. 'I don't understand how someone can hide their child like that. I have a two-year-old niece—Amy—and Johnnie hands out pictures of her to the family like they're fliers. Amy's first smile, Amy's first tooth, the first time Amy held a spoon—poor kid never gets a minute's peace.'

'It's not the same thing.'

'It should have been,' she argued.

Wasn't much he could do about that, was there? But while he didn't agree with the majority of choices his parents had made, he understood some of their motivation. 'Sometimes kids are better kept out of the public eye.'

'That's not what I'm talking about.' She scowled. 'Proud and protective aren't mutually exclusive.'

'Don't get mad, sweetheart. I agree with you.' He smiled, wondering if it had occurred to her the child she was so passionately defending was a fully grown man.

'Why aren't you angry?'

'It was a long time ago.'

'You *should* be angry.'

'You want to go dig him up so you can kick his ass?'

'Don't do that,' she said in an echo of the warning he'd given her. Twisting around, she grabbed a handful of his T-shirt and pushed her fist against his chest. 'That wasn't pity you could see, you idiot. I—'

'I get it.'

It was a lie. He didn't. But the way she was looking at him was tough enough to handle without asking what it meant. His reaction to the unknown emotion he could see in her eyes made the simple act of breathing in and out more difficult. Hadn't she got enough out of him for one day?

As if she'd heard the question, the hand on his arm slipped up to his shoulder and around the back of his neck, adding pressure to lower his mouth to hers. The contact was light, unbelievably sweet, whisper soft and Blake was amazed—considering how much of it they'd done—they could still find a kiss that was new.

When their lips parted and she looked into his eyes, his thoughts returned to what she'd yelled at him. He couldn't imagine her ever being messed up. Not the Liv he knew. Every time she dropped a piece of information into a conversation or during the meandering chatter she felt necessary to fill a silence, he'd been on it, tucking away each detail as if he was saving them for the proverbial rainy day. But what he knew wasn't enough. Not any more. Maybe that was why she'd pushed him.

Blake discovered he was okay with that.

'Can you tell me what happened six years ago?'

She nodded. 'I can talk about it. The compulsory visits to the department shrink can testify to that. He ticked the "not crazy" box—always good to know, right?'

Blake knew what she was doing. He was the master when it came to making light of things that weren't the remotest bit funny.

'You know my brothers are cops.'

'Yes.'

'Did I mention my dad was a cop?'

'No.'

'And his dad before him.' A wistful smile softened the blue of her eyes. 'It's in the blood. My whole life was geared towards becoming a cop. I couldn't wait to sign up.'

'How did your dad feel about that?'

'Mixed feelings, but I like to think he'd have been proud.' Avoiding his gaze, she added a matter-of-fact, 'He had a heart attack two years before I graduated from the academy.'

'He'd have been proud,' Blake said with certainty.

She flashed a small smile of appreciation before continuing. 'After graduation, rookies get partnered with a Training Officer. I got Nick. He taught me a lot. One of the things he kept saying was you can't be a cop if you let your emotions take over. We have to sit on them, push them deep inside so we can do our job. I struggled with that.'

But she'd learnt how to do it, hadn't she? It was a revealing insight into the woman he'd met at the beginning, while at the same time leaving him feeling as if he'd barely scratched the surface.

'I told you about needing to know someone's story to understand why they do the things they do.' She waited for his nod. 'What we're not supposed to do is help people make decisions.' She rolled her eyes. 'I still suck at that.'

'Little bit.' He smiled. 'But there's a difference between having an opinion and telling someone what to do.'

She raised a brow. 'Could we remember that the next time I have an opinion?'

Walked right into that one, hadn't he?

'We can try,' he allowed. Contrary to the impression he might have given her with rules that might possibly have been put there to see how long it would take her to break them, he was interested in her opinion. Didn't mean he had to agree with it or that she would change his mind, but he could make an effort to be less defensive. 'Keep going.'

There was a pause as she took another breath and held it for a long moment. 'On the patch we patrolled, there was an underpass at the edge of a park where homeless people gathered. We would drive by to check in on them. We looked for drug use and underage teens—kept an eye out if anyone was missing or died during the night—that kind of thing.' She shrugged. 'But you get to know people…'

'There's nothing wrong with that.'

'There is if you're struggling with the not getting

involved part of the job.' She sighed heavily. 'Every time we left, Nick had the same look on his face, especially after I got to know Jo. She was my contact. She would tell me when there had been problems, keep an eye on everyone, make sure anyone who couldn't make it to food handouts had something brought back to them. Jo was special—wise beyond her years in many ways.' She smiled. 'Still is...'

'You kept in touch with her?'

'We share an apartment.'

'Takes the phrase "bringing your work home with you" a tad too far, don't you think?'

'Don't judge,' she warned.

If she'd started adopting strays he was with Nick. How much could she realistically have known about the person she'd invited into her home? In a sense he supposed it was exactly what she'd done with him when she decided to share his bed. He frowned at the idea of being adopted like a stray. It was the last thing he wanted from her.

But since it begged the question of what he *did* want...

Her gaze lowered. 'Jo introduced me to Aiden. He was a good kid—messed up—but a good kid.' She blinked several times, as if focusing on something at a distance. 'When he had problems with a guy who was taking his stuff, I talked to him about it and suggested he try clearing the air. I got the usual lecture from Nick on the way to get coffee but he was right. While we were gone Aiden did what I'd suggested and talked to the guy. There was an argument—the guy pulled a knife—and Aiden was stabbed in the stomach. Took us less than ten minutes to get back when the call came in, but he died at the scene.'

When Blake felt another tremor run through her body, he tightened his arms. 'It wasn't your fault.'

'I wasn't holding the knife, but it felt like it was.'

'You made a suggestion. He didn't have to follow it.'

'I was wearing the uniform and he was an eighteen-year-old kid.' She shook her head. 'I should have known better. Or intervened—intervened would have been better…'

Except then she might have been the one who was stabbed in the stomach and died at the scene. Blake would never have met her. He didn't like that scenario.

'Bad things happen.' He frowned at how trite it sounded. 'You cared enough to try and help. I bet that meant a lot to a kid living on the streets.'

'It wasn't enough,' she said in a small voice.

Blake crooked his finger underneath her chin and tilted her face up, leaning down to look deep into her eyes as he repeated, *'It wasn't your fault.'*

'I know.'

'Do you?' He wasn't so sure.

'I want to.' She blinked incredulously. 'That's the first time I've admitted that. How did you know?'

'Guilt looks different on everyone. Same for grief.' He may have been struggling to deal with his inability to feel either one, 'But I know them when I see them.'

'I'm better now, really I am,' she reassured him. 'It just takes time to work through it, you know?'

He brushed the backs of his fingers across her jaw. 'I know, but you can't blame yourself, Liv. We all make choices every day—some big, some small. If we tried to figure out the chain reaction of every single one, we'd go crazy. We won't always get everything right but we can learn from the mistakes and decide what we're willing to live with when we look in the mirror. I don't think anyone can do anything more than that.'

Her brows lifted. 'Wow—that's actually quite—'

'Smart?'

'I was going to say insightful.'

'You could try looking less surprised.' When he smiled and she smiled back at him, he tucked a strand of hair behind her ear before he lowered his arm. 'So is that why you quit?'

'It was the start of it.' She nodded. 'When you're a rookie you know stuff like that is going to happen. Everyone has a bad shift; it's part of the job. But it wasn't one bad shift. They just kept on coming. You think you'll handle it. I didn't. The first time I drew my weapon my hands were shaking.' She looked down and folded her fingers into her palms. 'That's when I knew I was done.'

'And went to Law School…'

'Took me a while to figure it out.' She smiled again. 'But it seemed like a logical move when I thought about it.'

Blake couldn't remember ever respecting anyone as much as he respected Liv at that moment. He knew what it took to pick up, dust down and move on but he'd never known what it took to stand still and regroup the way she had. Possibly because he'd never had anything to fight for—at least nothing that mattered to him as much as the oath she'd taken to 'Protect and Serve'.

Because she was still doing it, wasn't she?

Apart from her concern for the thousands of little guys employed by Warren Enterprises, Blake realised she'd been doing it with him. More than simply serving her position as his lawyer, her opinion was offered—even when he didn't want to hear it—to allow him to see things from a different perspective. If she thought he was wrong, she challenged him, protecting him from the kind of clouded judgement that could get in the way. She was right about that—it had done, more than once in his life, but he wouldn't let it happen with her. He was determined to give her what she wanted. No regrets, only bittersweet memories.

'Thank you—' it was something he should have said before, for more than one reason, but this time '—for telling me.'

'You're welcome.' The blue of her eyes softened with warmth that reached deep inside him, wrapping around the emptiness the way it did when they made love.

Gaze roving over her face, he took in all of the familiar details he still found fascinating. What was it about her that was different from any of the women he'd met before? With Liv, he felt things more intensely: desire, need, hunger. He was frustrated at his inability to give her more than a sexual relationship and that warred with new sensations of jealousy, possessiveness and a newfound protectiveness he felt towards her—even if it meant protecting her from *him*.

Someone with the ability to care as much as she could shouldn't be around someone like him. Not if the emptiness he carried would lead to him leeching emotion from her in an attempt to fill the void. If he thought for a second that might happen he would have to let her go sooner rather than later, whether he was ready to or not.

'You hungry?' she asked, letting him off the hook when it came to his part of the sharing bargain they'd made.

He was okay about that, not because he didn't want to make the effort to talk to her, but because she was right. Even if talking about it helped—which he doubted—it wasn't all about him. Nor should it be.

'Yes.' He smiled with meaning.

'I meant for food.'

He grinned. 'That, too.'

'You're insatiable, you know that, don't you?' She got to her feet and reached for his hands to pull him up.

'Is that a complaint?'

'Did it sound like a complaint?'

Smile becoming a grin as they walked down the hall, he nudged his upper arm off her shoulder and rocked her sideways. 'So it's another *compliment…*'

'It's amazing to me the size of that head doesn't topple you over.'

CHAPTER ELEVEN

'I THINK you should keep this house. It *needs you.*'

'I don't think it's particular about who looks after it so long as someone does. Houses can be funny that way.'

Walking hand in hand along the beach, Olivia took a long breath and smiled. She was happy, closer to Blake since their breakthrough than was sensible, admittedly, but the way she looked at it, a girl had to grab moments of happiness where she could find them, even if part of her was waiting for a pinprick to burst the bubble they were living in.

She tilted her chin and looked up at him. 'Did I point out the advantage of it being in The Hamptons?'

'No, but you're going to.'

'You wouldn't have to be here the whole year round. Most people aren't.' She continued smiling. 'And when you get itchy feet, it's not like you don't still have plenty of places to go. You own places all over the world now.'

'And a choice of private jets to take me there…'

'Precisely.'

'I'd be happy to help you join the Mile High Club.'

'I'm serious.' She laughed.

'So am I.' He winked.

When she rolled her eyes, he stopped and leaned down to kiss her—firm, practised lips drawing a hum of approval from low in her throat. It was a gentle, almost tender kiss—one that had been happening more frequently since he'd started sharing little details of his life with her—but it wasn't always like that with them. There were times it was all about hunger and need, times when it was more about giving than taking, times when it was teasing and times—like this—when it soothed and said everything was going to be all right. Even if she knew it wouldn't.

If she hadn't already known, when he told her about some of the places he'd lived, the people he'd met and she watched his eyes shine with memories she was reminded how different they were. Blake was a rolling stone, free of ties and the burden of any responsibilities beyond taking care of himself, while Olivia was tethered to the people she loved and the place she called home. She was a New Yorker, a Brannigan, a best friend and a lawyer who put long hours into her work—she didn't even know where a relationship with a man like Blake would fit into that. And knowing she'd be willing to find out took a little of the brightness off her day…

'Just think about it,' she mumbled against his mouth.

Leaning back, he used his free hand to brush her hair from her cheek. 'You really love this place.'

'I do.'

He searched her eyes before announcing, 'It's yours.'

A low huff of disbelieving laughter left her lips. 'You can't give me a house.'

'I can do what I want.'

Reaching up, she wrapped her fingers around his hand, lowering it from her face as her smile faded. 'I can't accept a gift that large from you.'

'Yes, you can.'

'No, I can't.' The second huff of laughter was tighter. 'People don't give other people houses.'

'Not like I don't have plenty to spare, is it?'

'Stop it,' she said more firmly, stepping back. 'I'm just saying you should think about it before selling it. Not every decision you make has to be made in a hurry. Some things are worth hanging on to…'

When he frowned at the words, she let go of his hands and turned away, walking ahead of him while berating herself for giving him the impression she wanted more than they had. As obvious as it was she hadn't known the risk she was taking emotionally when she slept with him, when it came to commitment she knew exactly where she stood. What they had would end. It was simply a matter of when.

Why did she have to keep reminding herself of that?

'It's just a house, Liv.'

'You keep saying that.' She turned and walked backwards for a few steps. 'It's not *just* a house and even if it was, I would still feel the same way. I don't want expensive gifts from you. It would feel like—'

A large hand captured her elbow when she turned away, holding her in place as he stepped closer. 'Payment?'

Frustration threaded her voice. 'It's how it might look. *There she goes—the lawyer who slept with a billionaire and got a house in The Hamptons out of it.*'

'I don't care what people think.'

'I do,' she said in a softer voice. 'We're judged by our actions. How can I work with rich and powerful company owners in the future if they suspect my motives? I won't be able to smile at a guy without someone thinking I'm out to get something.'

'They won't think that.'

'They might.'

The hold on her arm loosened, his thumb brushing over her skin. 'I can't give you anything? Flowers, chocolates—

all the usual stuff women are supposed to like—they're all out of bounds, are they?'

A smile hovered around the corners of her mouth. 'I didn't say *that.* What I'm saying is there's a gap the size of the Grand Canyon between a bunch of flowers and a house. You don't have to woo me, Blake. Considering how much time we've spent in bed, I think it's safe to say we skipped the wooing part, wouldn't you?'

'I don't even know what it means.'

Taking a step forward, Olivia laid a palm on his chest. 'I don't need expensive gifts from you—anyone who does isn't worth your time.'

What he didn't know was how great a gift he'd already given her. When she'd told him what happened in the past, he'd done more than tell her what she'd needed to hear. While she'd thought she'd moved on, she realised she hadn't let that day go—carrying the memory of it around with her like a penance. But while talking to him without getting upset, hearing the sincerity in his rough voice and seeing the resolve in his eyes when he told her it wasn't her fault, she'd felt some of the weight being lifted from her shoulders. The department shrink, who had expected her to spend hours reliving the moment Aiden died, people she'd worked with, family and friends—none of them had been able to do that for her. Then along came Blake.

As frightening as it was that he'd seen inside her to something she hadn't admitted to herself, by understanding what had happened he'd given her a gift money could never buy: the first hint of real peace of mind she'd felt in six years.

He shook his head. 'Still doing it, aren't you?'

'Doing what?'

'Preparing me for a new life…'

'Your life *is* different. I think you know that now.' Her gaze searched his eyes, sincerity lacing her voice. 'Sometimes we don't get to choose where we end up. Stuff happens. You'll find something good you can take out of this, I know you will. You've just got to be open to it.'

'What makes you think I haven't done that already?'

Flashing a smile to cover the sudden ache in her chest, she rocked onto her toes and placed a kiss on the corner of his mouth. 'You can be incredibly sweet when you set your mind to it.'

'Don't go telling anyone.'

'Your secret's safe with me.'

Blake circled her with his arms, drawing her close, her body fitting into his in a way that suggested they'd been together for a lot longer than they had. In turn, she wrapped her arms around his lean waist, placed her cheek on his chest and listened to the steady beat of his heart, drawing comfort from the sound.

Sad thing was—if things had been different—she knew he was exactly the kind of man she needed in her life. Despite the things they both still held back, having someone she could lean on during moments when she got tired of being strong, and who could find the words to make her feel like less of an emotional ticking time bomb, sounded pretty darn good to her. She just wished she could find a way of helping him the way he'd helped her.

Blinking as she looked at the sparkling ocean, she took a mental snapshot of the moment and stored it away in her memory for the day he wouldn't be there any more. She didn't want to leave. Not yet. As if somehow she knew when they left The Hamptons it was the beginning of the end.

'We'll forget I tried to give you a house,' his deep, rough

edged voice rumbled above her head. 'Be a bitch to gift-wrap anyway.'

'It would.' She smiled.

When she leaned back to look at him, he lowered his mouth to hers for one of the kisses that lit a flame inside her body. She'd been wrong about the attraction between them flaring and fizzling out. If anything, knowing him better had added a depth and richness to their lovemaking that hadn't been there before. She wanted him *more*, not less. Making love and sharing the moment when they were at their most vulnerable, falling asleep next to him and waking up in his arms—she knew she would miss it when it was gone. He'd be a hard act to follow, too.

'We should probably think about packing.' She sighed with regret, loosening the arms around his waist and backing away. 'The chopper will be here first thing.'

'We still have time.'

'I don't want to leave a mess behind.' She forced a smile to hide any subliminal message he might read into the words. 'You were the one who told the staff we could fend for ourselves, remember?'

Hand held in his again, they headed back up the beach in a silence she didn't feel the need to fill.

'I won't sell it,' he said before they left the sand.

'I'm glad.' Wrapping her arms around his waist again, she clung to his side, his arm draped across her shoulder as she added, 'If you're lucky, next time I'm in The Hamptons, I might look you up.'

'You're gonna call first, right?'

Blake settled back against the pillows, lifting his arm so Liv could curl in beside him before she fell asleep. As her cheek rubbed against his chest, her breasts smooshed against his side, he found himself staring across the room, fingers tracing lazy circles on her back while he thought.

It wasn't the first time he'd found himself focusing on the mental picture she'd helped create of the house he'd told her he would keep. She was right, changes could be made—some of them he would probably enjoy making. Old houses had always been his thing, after all. Not that he'd ever had one he could call his own, but he suspected it would add to the sense of pride he put into his work. But while mentally working his way from room to room, thinking about the changes, Liv was always there. He couldn't imagine it without her.

But even if he had it in him to put down roots, there were no guarantees. Especially when staying put would mean making decisions he hadn't wanted to make—ones he knew would put him in a perpetually foul mood until he worked his way through them. Not wanting to run the company wasn't just the issue of responsibility. Much as it killed him to admit it, part of the problem was—*maybe*—he didn't think he could. If there was one thing Blake hated more than finding something he wasn't any good at, it was being surrounded by people who were better at it than him.

But he could delegate. He'd been known to allocate work to guys who knew what they were doing. Wasn't that kind of the same thing as running a company? But considering doing something he would enjoy—like renovating the warehouse—was one thing, making changes that large to his life was another. *Why was he even thinking about it?*

Liv moved her calf against his leg, her murmur of contentment calming him. He remembered the first morning in his apartment when he'd felt better with her close to him. Then he thought about how it felt worse when the distance between them increased. She was the equivalent of an open fire in the depths of winter. Step too close and flames would consume him, licking his body and igniting his senses until he exploded in a shower of white heat and bright light. Step too far back and he could find himself standing in arctic temperatures that seeped into his bones, numbing him until he wouldn't have the strength to step close to the warmth again.

Was that how it would feel when she wasn't there?

Just the thought of walking away from her made him keenly aware of the cold empty place inside him. He needed to deal with that—plunge into the middle of it and get to the heart of why he couldn't feel anything about the death of the man who had contributed half his DNA. He couldn't stay numb for ever or get angry every time he was faced with something he couldn't communicate clearly. Hadn't talking to Liv the last couple of days proved he could find words if he made the effort?

'We moved around a lot...'

He wanted her to know—to understand why staying in one place and putting down roots was something he knew nothing about.

'It started when I was seven. A guy turned up outside school and argued with my mom. He followed us home, parked outside the house, took pictures.' He felt the blink of Liv's lashes against his chest as he spoke. 'When none of that got him anywhere he hung around at recess, calling me from the other side of the fence, "Hey kid, where's your dad? Ever meet him? I've got a picture—you want to see?"'

Blake could still hear the man's voice and remember what it felt like to see the picture—the sense of curiosity and a childlike awe. 'It was the first time I'd laid eyes on Charlie Warren. I'd hit that age where I was starting to ask the questions kids ask when they notice they don't have two parents. My mom would tell me he was busy or had important stuff to do—how his job made him responsible for lots of other folks. Sometimes she'd just change the subject. Guess it wasn't easy to explain to a kid why you loved someone but couldn't stay with them.'

Pausing to take a breath, he checked to see how he felt about that. When he was a kid it had hurt and made him think his dad didn't care, but now, nothing.

'Within twenty-four hours of seeing the photo we were packed and headed to a new town.' He remembered being angry, not wanting to leave his friends or his school and arguing with his mom until she'd promised him the dog he wanted so badly. They'd never got a dog.

'My mom was always looking over her shoulder after that. Maybe she was right and there were others. After a while, I think it was paranoia. Nobody cared who we were.'

'He was a reporter?' Liv asked in a soft voice.

'Yes.'

'She was protecting you.'

'The only way she knew how. It's why she left Charlie. She couldn't handle the spotlight—didn't want me under it either—finding out she was pregnant made her decision.'

'How many times did you move when you were a kid?'

'I stopped counting. At first, you think it's how everyone lives. By the time you're old enough to know better, you don't know anything else.' He breathed deep, feeling a hint of remembered acceptance. 'When the reporter lost our trail, he headed straight for Charlie to break the news to him he had a kid. Charlie hired a PI to track us down. Gotta give it to him, he had one hell of a stand-up row with my mom when he found us.'

'You'd have done the same thing.'

He would, but he'd never understood how Charlie might have felt until that moment. In the darkness, he could feel the curve of Liv's stomach pressed against his waist and for a moment—before he'd realised what he was doing—he pictured what it would be like to have a full, rounded belly pressed against him and a baby—*their baby*—moving inside her. Stepping into Charlie's shoes and replacing his mom with Liv, he understood how angry his father had been at his mother for keeping his child from him. Liv was right, he'd have yelled, too. He'd have yelled his damn head off.

But the mental image he'd created didn't stop there.

The heated weight in his groin at the thought of what was involved when it came to putting a baby in Liv was hardly a surprise, but what stunned him was how completely okay he was with the idea of her being pregnant with his child, of a new life that would bind them together. He'd never thought about having kids, about a family of his own.

That suddenly he thought—

'Keep going,' she coaxed in the same soft, totally-unaware-of-his-thoughts voice.

'Where was I?' It took a lot to keep his voice even, and Blake didn't know how she couldn't hear his heart racing, his body already kicking into full-on baby-making mode. What the hell was *that* about?

'Charlie found you. He had a fight with your mom.'

Lifting the hand from her back, he swiped it over his face in an attempt to pull himself together. 'When they'd calmed down and talked about it, I think Charlie got it. He'd hit a few reporters in his time and he knew how insecure my mom was. He loved her. Guess he must have, since he never married. So they made a deal. She'd send him pictures and keep him updated—he'd send money and keep the secret till I was old enough to decide what I wanted.'

'He didn't visit?'

'When he could—wasn't always easy for him to keep a low profile. Don't think he found it easy to keep track of us at times, either. My mom could be hit-and-miss with the whole stay in touch part of the deal. Every time he visited she was borderline manic for days after he left. Everyone was looking at us, everyone was talking about us; someone had to have recognised Charlie. It was easier when he didn't visit.' Blake had known that at twelve. He'd resented the man who made life more difficult for him than it already was. 'Not like a handful of days a few times a year was gonna make for much of a father/son bond, anyway. Once I hit my teens, he didn't stand a chance. I wasn't interested in why he wasn't there. Bottom line, he wasn't and I had my mom to deal with on my own.'

'Did she ever get help?'

'Talk to someone who might rat us out? *Hell, no.*' And by the time he'd worked out that his mom might have benefited from talking things through with someone it had been too late. 'If she'd visited a doctor more often they might have found the tumours sooner.'

He'd felt guilty about that. He should have made her go sooner, should have known there was something wrong.

'Is that when you came here?'

'When she collapsed and the hospital emergency room said it was cancer, I made her contact Charlie to pull some strings and get her the treatment she needed.' His pride might have been dented but it had been her only hope. 'After a couple of semesters at high school in New York, they decided I'd spend the summer here. I wasn't given a choice. It didn't go the way I think Charlie hoped it would. By seventeen I had attitude, was getting into trouble, resented the hell out of being here and was stuck with a guy I barely knew. Not like we could toss a football around. He was a lot older than my mom, to begin with.'

Blake ran his palm along her spine before starting to make circles with his fingertips again. 'Looking back, I think it took that summer and the couple of years my mom was sick before she died to straighten me out. If things had been different, there might have been more than one member of the Warren family wearing an orange jumpsuit.'

'I don't think so,' Liv said with a certainty he far from deserved.

She hadn't known him.

'When was the last time you saw him?'

'Her funeral.'

'He didn't try to get in touch again?'

Blake immediately thought of the envelope he'd been carrying around. 'Not till it was too late.'

'He should have tried.'

'I can be pig-headed when I set my mind to it.'

'You?' She pressed a kiss to the skin directly over his heart and rubbed her cheek against his chest. *'Never.'*

He smiled into the darkness.

They stayed silent for a long while after that, a clock chiming the hour somewhere in the distance while Blake tried to make sense of his thoughts. What the hell was he doing thinking about having a child when he had no idea what family meant? Families were something other people had. Granted, it might explain some of the emptiness he carried around, but what if having a family of his own didn't fill it or, worse still, he handed whatever defect it was inside him onto his kids? They didn't deserve that. Neither did their mother. His arms tightened instinctively around Liv. He wouldn't do that to her.

The void within him expanding, he vowed he would let her go before he came close to hurting her. He could do the honourable thing. What he couldn't do was be selfish, give her half a man or one who might some day succumb to the emptiness and leave her living with a shell. A wave of anger crashed over him. It wasn't enough, damn it.

He wasn't enough *for her.*

As if sensing he needed to get lost in her again, she shifted and stretched her body along the length of his, her hands smoothing up his arms and across his shoulders as she whispered, 'Thank you. For telling me…'

It felt like the least he could do. His inability to give her something more when nothing ever felt like enough forced him to fight his most basic instincts and remain passive while she took what she wanted. But as her soft lips moved across his mouth he felt himself drawn to her warmth, the need to move closer to the fire making him roll them over so he could set the pace before he was engulfed by the flames she ignited inside him.

He couldn't get enough of her. Maybe he never would.

Olivia found the letter by accident as she picked up a pair of his jeans. When it dropped to the floor, she bent down to lift it without thinking, unfolding it to see if she could toss it away. Reading several familiar scored out addresses, she froze, turning it over and checking the sender's address above the unbroken seal. How long had he been carrying it around? She checked the date on the postmarks, her brows lifting in surprise.

'How many damn bottles of stuff did you bring with you?' Blake called from the bathroom.

'You think I look this good without any effort?' she called back while frowning at the envelope.

'That's one of those questions there's no right answer to, right?'

Turning towards the bed where their weekend bags were laid out, she debated telling him she'd found it. She loved that he'd shared so much with her but the closer she felt to him, the more there was to lose. The story of his past told in the deep, rough rumble of his voice while he'd held her in the dark had had even more of an effect on her than the fact they'd made love in what had felt like the truest sense of the word.

But why hadn't he opened it? Why carry it around? Why hadn't he told her—?

Lifting her chin, she frowned harder. Just because her heart longed to pour everything she had to give—without restraint—on someone who might need her a fraction as much as she needed him, didn't mean she could throw caution to the wind and go looking for something with Blake that wasn't there. How many times did she need to remember what they had would end before it sank in? Folding the envelope between her thumb and forefinger, she pushed it back into the pocket of his jeans, packing them into his bag as he appeared beside her and dumped an armful of assorted toiletries into hers.

'Is there anything left in Macy's?'

'Remind me never to show you my shoe closet.'

'I'm allowed to give you shoes, am I?'

'I think you'll find that's enabling an addict.' When he shook his head and leaned down to kiss her, she turned her cheek. 'Helicopter's here. We should go.'

It wasn't a lie—she could hear the rhythmical beat of the rotors close by—but the fact she'd taken a step away from him—no matter how small or practical the rejection might have seemed—made Blake frown.

'What's wrong?'

'Apart from the fact I seem to be packing for you?'

'The house will still be here a week from now,' he said in the rough voice she loved so much. 'We'll come back at the weekend.'

Olivia tucked a strand of hair behind her ear before

pulling the zips on the bags. 'I can't next weekend. It's Jo's birthday.'

'We'll be back, Liv.'

'You never know.' She tossed her best imitation of a smile at him as she began filling in the cracks in the wall around her heart. 'Might be another place we like better.'

'Not fooling anyone in this room, sweetheart.' Picking up their bags, he pressed a kiss into her hair. 'I refuse to feel jealous of a house.'

The helicopter was swinging in to land by the time they got to the front door, Blake jogging down the steps with their bags and walking across the gravel with long, confident strides as Olivia reached out a hand to the wooden railing and looked up.

''Bye, house.' She swallowed to loosen the sudden knot in her throat. 'Take care of him for me.'

Knowing he'd never had a place to call home made him a perfect fit for a house calling out to be loved. It might be a part-time relationship, but while he was there she knew he would lavish attention on it in a way that could last more than a lifetime.

Turning, she forced reluctant legs to carry her away. Now they were leaving The Hamptons and fantasy land, it was time for a reality check. Holding her head up, she walked towards the helicopter without looking back.

She'd never considered she would be the one to end it. She wondered why. Was she so desperate to hang on to every last moment until the day he walked away? How much of a masochist did that make her?

Enough was enough. It was time for damage control. She had to give herself a fighting chance of getting over him—something she doubted would be easy, especially if she fell in love with more than his house.

CHAPTER TWELVE

'I ALWAYS figured if someone handed me a few million bucks I'd look happier than you do right now.' Marty dropped onto the stool next to him and ordered a beer.

'Not all it's cracked up to be,' Blake replied.

It earned him a grin, 'Aw, you're just saying that to make me feel better.'

No, he wasn't. He'd been right about making decisions he hadn't planned on making putting him in a perpetually foul mood. The fact Liv was being weird with him wasn't helping any either. Why hadn't she kicked him to the kerb for his attitude of late? It wasn't like her.

'Punishment for being economical with the truth, if you ask me,' Marty said.

Blake tilted his bottle to his mouth. 'You knew my old man had money and I wanted nothing to do with it.'

'Left out the Charles Warren part, didn't we, Anders?'

'Could we knock it off with the Anders some time soon?'

The baseball game playing on a large screen behind the bar took up their attention while some of the lunchtime crowd filtered in, Marty eventually taking a short breath before stepping into touchy territory again.

'So how was your first day at the office?'

'I'm just looking around.'

'Well, while you were—' he made speech marks with his fingers '— "looking around", the rest of the class took a field trip to that warehouse down by the river.'

Blake turned towards him. 'And?'

'Doable.' Marty nodded. 'You'll need to clear those changes you want made with the architect and building control, but yeah—should keep us busy for a while.'

'Good. Bring in as many new guys as you need.'

'Yes, Boss.'

Blake shook his head. 'Don't do that.'

They watched the game for a while, Marty glancing sideways when Blake kept checking the screen of his cell-phone. 'Waiting on an important call?'

'No.' He set the phone down and lifted his beer.

'So what's the problem?'

'Apart from the fact I might need a new lawyer?'

If firing her was what it took to make it feel as if they could hold a conversation that didn't involve work, then so be it. Seemed to Blake they'd talked about little else since they got back to Manhattan. But as sexy as he found her, he didn't want to spend time with the lawyer—he wanted to spend it with the woman he'd been with in The Hamptons. Where the hell had *she* gone? He missed her.

'Thought there was something going on with you two.'

Blake frowned as he swallowed.

'Ah,' Marty said.

They sat in silence for as long as Blake could stand it. 'You got something to say, spit it out.'

'It's none of my business.'

'Never stopped you before…'

'Never looked like it mattered before…'

There were loud groans and shouts of complaint in reaction to what was happening on-screen while Blake focused his gaze on the bottle he was turning in circles with his hands. 'It matters.'

There was a long pause, then Marty dived in with, 'Know what I think?'

'I will when you get round to spitting it out.'

'I think you stepped out of the dugout too soon.' He nodded. 'Didn't help any that they sent a curve ball your way with the lady lawyer.'

Blake glanced at him from the corner of his eye. 'Could we do this without the baseball analogies?'

Leaning an elbow on the bar as the game went to commercial, Marty turned towards him. 'Knee-jerk reaction has always been your problem. We've both known that since high school. First day you turned up, you came out swinging and asked questions later. That's what you've done this time. You ask me, you didn't spend enough time prepping for the game. One look at her and you were stepping up to the plate. Understandable—you got eyes—but now you're asking questions and I'm willing to bet some of them you should have asked yourself earlier.'

As the game resumed on the screen, he turned away, leaving Blake to absorb what he'd said. 'Didn't occur to you to say any of this sooner?'

'Ain't nobody getting in your way when you come out swinging.'

'Didn't stop you that first day in high school…'

Marty shrugged again. 'You were taking on half the football team. Someone had to stop you getting killed.'

'I didn't know she was dating the quarterback.'

'Yeah—' he snorted sarcastically into the rim of his beer bottle '—'cos cheerleaders didn't date football players in any of the two hundred other schools you went to. That pretty much *never* happens.'

Breathing deep, Blake looked up at the screen. Marty

was right, he *was* asking questions. Some he'd thought he knew the answers to. Some he'd never asked before. Some it stunned him he even *had* to ask. As to the part about Liv being the reason he'd stepped up to the plate before he was ready? That was probably true, too. He'd wanted her from the moment he laid eyes on her. Still did. Except now he wanted more at a time when he was pretty certain she was backing off. But since he'd never stuck around long enough for a woman to back off before he did, how would he know?

'Had to happen some time,' Marty commented.

'What did?'

'Something to make you think about staying put.'

They sat in silence through two sets of commercials, occasionally lifting their bottles and tilting them to their mouths while Blake tore the corner off the label and rolled it between his fingertips.

'What's it like?' he asked, tossing the paper ball onto the bar and watching it roll away.

'What's what like?'

'Staying put.'

'Depends what you want.' Marty reached across for a handful of mini pretzels. 'And who you want it with.'

That helped.

'You see your life without her in it?'

Blake frowned at the question and got a nod in reply.

'Don't suppose you counted up how long you'd been here before all this happened.' Marty shook his head. 'No. Give it a minute. Use fingers and toes.'

'We'd been busy.'

'We had plenty of work the last two times you came home and it didn't stop you getting itchy feet after six months.' He tossed another pretzel in his mouth and chewed while talking. 'Happens to the best of us—just comes a time when we're ready to put down roots and settle.'

'You got married at *nineteen*.'

'Some of us get lucky earlier than others.' He glanced sideways. 'No one said anything about you getting married, did they?'

Blake clenched his teeth together hard enough to make his jaw ache.

'Mmm.' Marty quirked his brows as he looked up at the screen. 'Might want to figure out how serious you are about her before that reporter comes sniffing around again. He seemed as interested in her as he was in you.'

'*What* reporter?'

'Olivia Brannigan?'

'Yes.' She looked up at the fair-haired man, tucking away the phone she'd been checking for messages as a manila envelope appeared at eye-level.

'I'd like to talk to you about Blake Clayton.'

'And you are?'

'Ed Parnell, freelance reporter.'

Pressing her lips together, Olivia lowered her chin and turned her attention to the remnants of a Waldorf salad. 'I have nothing to say to you, Mr Parnell.'

'You might when you look at the pictures.'

Glancing at the envelope while she wiped her hands with a paper napkin, Olivia reasoned it would be better to know what she was dealing with. It was part of her job as Blake's lawyer, would be remiss of her not to—

Who was she kidding? Of course she was going to look.

Taking the envelope from him, she twisted the tab and slid out the contents, frowning as she flicked through photograph after photograph. Blake kissing her at the heliport on the way to The Hamptons, the two of them laughing at something as they walked along a sidewalk—there were even pictures of her leaving his apartment.

It felt as if something had been stolen from them.

'Your boyfriend is newsworthy. Secret son of famous billionaire inherits entire family fortune?' The young man smiled. 'Rags to riches stories, people love them.'

'I think we're done here.' Lifting the salad container and her empty coffee cup, she pushed to her feet and dropped them into a nearby trashcan. She walked past the fountain and along the dappled path that took her out of the park and into the crowd.

The reporter followed her. 'I'm sure Warren Enterprises shareholders will be fascinated by his plans for the company now he's the majority shareholder. Especially when we take into consideration he's a carpenter. How many carpenters do you think there are running multinational companies, Ms Brannigan?'

'No comment.'

Taking her sunglasses off her head to hide her eyes, she frowned as she headed for the crossing. How dare he suggest Blake wasn't capable of running the company? That man was capable of anything if he set his mind to it. When he wanted something—well, she *knew*, didn't she?

If he ever met a woman he could love, she wouldn't have a single doubt how he felt. Nothing would stand in his way. The woman wouldn't stand a chance. She might put up a fight—he could be annoying as hell—but if he let her, she would see what was standing right in front of her and when she did she would hold on tight and never want to let go.

They would find a way to make it work, *together*.

Olivia had never been as jealous as she was of the imaginary woman who might one day share his life. If he was capable of staying in one place and wanted her as much as she wanted him—

As if thinking about him could conjure him up out of nowhere… She blinked. At first he was just a figure moving towards her in the distance, among a great many others doing the same thing; the fact she'd even noticed was a miracle in itself considering the volume of people on the streets of Manhattan. A second later he was a man. Then a tall man with broad shoulders and unruly chocolate-brown hair who became a stand-out-of-the-crowd, unbearably sexy male with his dark, intense gaze fixed on her and an expression that said nothing and no one was getting in his way.

It was a cruel glimpse of something she hadn't been ready to admit she needed more than her next breath.

As the world contracted, Olivia froze, the wall around her heart crumbling to dust and emotion gushing into her chest. How could she have been so blind? She'd thought it wouldn't be easy to get over him *if* she fell in love with him? There was no *if* about it.

The shaking started in her midriff and radiated outwards over her body, forcing her to clamp her teeth together to stop them from chattering as she experienced the closest thing she'd ever had to a panic attack.

'Will he be optioning shares? I've heard he's been selling off properties. Care to comment on that?'

Blake's gaze shifted sharply to the reporter as he pushed up the sleeves of his dark blue shirt.

'Where has he been all these years? How come nobody has heard of him? Did Charles Warren hide the fact he had a child on purpose—because of the mother, maybe?'

Five strides away. Four, three… His large hands bunched into fists.

'Then we get to you, Ms Brannigan. Nothing like a little

romance to add to the story. When I realised your relationship was more than professional, I did a little research. You used to be with the NYPD. Is it true a homeless teenager died in your arms?'

Blake came to a halt in front of her and glared at the younger man, who took a step back in surprise.

'Mr Clayton, I'm glad you're here,' he said warily as Olivia silently handed over the envelope.

'I'd hold that thought if I were you,' Blake replied ominously as he looked at the photographs.

Summoning every ounce of the control she'd learnt in the last six years, Olivia stepped between them, the professional warning the client, 'Don't say anything.'

She reached up a hand and placed her sunglasses back on her head. She sized up the younger man with a cursory glance. 'Mr Parnell, I think I should warn you, continue stalking my client, I'll slap a restraining order on you so fast you'll be lucky not to be arrested in the next ten minutes for violating it. Print so much as one word that could be considered defamation of character, I will also sue for libel—and when I say "sue" I mean your great-great-grandchildren will still be paying off the debt.'

'You can't—'

'Yes, I can.' She smiled coldly, the chill washing over her body turning her blood to ice in her veins. 'What's more, *I'll enjoy it.*'

He opened and closed his mouth a couple of times.

Olivia raised a brow. 'You realise you'd be taking on one of the largest, most reputable law firms in Manhattan along with one of the richest men in the country?'

His eyes tightened. 'I'm not done.'

'Yes, you are,' Blake said.

The reporter looked at him, baulked at his expression

and beat a hasty retreat. As he did, Olivia took a short breath. 'He won't be the last.'

'I know.'

'Are you ready for that?'

'As ready as I'll ever be.'

Considering the effect it had on his life the last time anyone attempted to make a story out of him, she suspected it was something he would never be comfortable with—she knew *she* wasn't. But she wasn't his mother. She would fight with every weapon in her arsenal and hunt down every slimy, headline-grabbing, muck-racking, gossip-mongering—

'You can't hit them,' she said. 'They'll sue.'

'Be worth every cent.'

'They get more of a story out of it that way.'

He frowned. 'You shouldn't have got pulled into it.'

'It's hard to deny photographic evidence.'

'Will it be a problem for you at work?'

'Nothing I can't handle,' she hoped, but if her entire world crumbled around her ears again she would have no one to blame but herself.

Blake's voice lowered to a rough rumble. 'You didn't tell me he died in your arms.'

Gaze fixed on a random point just past his left ear, Olivia fought to keep her vulnerable emotions out of sight. She couldn't do what she had to do if there was so much as a hint of how she felt visible to him. The fact he'd always been able to see beyond the surface meant she had to draw on acting skills at an award-winning level. But he hadn't asked her to fall in love with him. She would let him go before she had to listen to him tell her they were done.

'You were covered in blood, weren't you?'

'Stomach wounds bleed like a bitch,' she said flatly.

'Don't do that.'

She shrugged. 'It's true.'

'Okay, that's it. I've had enough.' Grasping hold of her hand, he led her back to the park, turning to face her when he'd found a quiet corner. 'What's going on, Liv? And don't tell me it has something to do with that reporter. We both know that's not true. Whatever it is started when we left the house in The Hamptons—so what is it?'

Staring at his shirt while mentally preparing herself, her gaze lifted, button by button, over his open collar, the column of his neck, his tense jawline and the curve of his delicious lower lip until she was looking into the dark eyes she loved so much. She could do this, even if—for a moment—she was angry she had to and rallied against it.

'We both knew this was coming.' She slipped her hand free, curling her fingers into her palm to capture the warmth of their last touch.

'Knew what was coming?'

'The firm has a couple of important litigation cases coming up.' She was lying through her teeth, but she managed to hold his gaze. 'One of my associates familiar with Warren Enterprises subsidiaries will be taking over your case.'

Blake looked as angry as he'd been with the reporter. 'I can choose my own damn lawyer.'

'Naturally, we hope you stay with the firm…'

'Seriously—' he jerked his brows '—that's how you're handling this?'

'You're right; things haven't been the same since we got back to the city.' She could be honest about that. Turned out making the decision to end things and actually going through with it were two entirely different things. She hadn't wanted to let go, had been greedy and hung on for a few more memories while ignoring the reason she felt that way.

'I think it better we call it a day.' She avoided his gaze when it got difficult to keep up the pretence as she tried to figure out how long she'd been in love with him. It might have been lust at first sight, but the moment she'd started smiling when he wasn't there should have warned her of the potential danger. 'There's no point dragging it out till things get ugly.'

'Absolutely, best not drag it out till *that* happens.'

Her gaze slid swiftly back to his. 'What do you want me to say?'

'An explanation would be nice.'

'We both knew what we were getting into.'

'Did we?'

Had the fact she was using *his* reasoning escaped him? Olivia frowned, emotion churning frantically inside her chest. 'You may be tied up in Warren Enterprises business right now but we both know when you're done you'll move on. It's what you do. I knew that before I met you.'

She wasn't telling him anything he didn't already know. She remembered him talking about working with wood, how he did not know whether a piece would be worth keeping until he got below the surface. That wasn't the case for them. When she got beneath the surface she didn't get to choose whether to keep it or toss it away. She was being *forced* to toss it away. Spending each day waiting for the time to come when he would get restless and want to move on would cause her heart to shrivel up a little more with each passing hour, haemorrhaging emotion, bleeding her dry.

'You better be damn certain this is what you want.' His mouth twisted into a cruel impersonation of a smile. 'In case you hadn't noticed, I'm not big on looking back.'

'Don't make me the bad guy in this,' she warned. 'No one's to blame here. We have to be realistic. I know what I'm doing.'

'Beating me to the punch?'

Olivia was hanging on to her control by a thin thread. 'Can you tell me you won't walk at some point?'

'*Liv...*' For a second he looked pained.

'Tell me you won't get restless a month from now, or two months or six.' She wished he could. But she couldn't change him. She didn't want to, not really. If he wasn't the man he was, she wouldn't have fallen for him.

'You think I wouldn't *try* to stay—*for you*?'

'That's just it, Blake. You shouldn't feel you have to do it for me.' She almost choked on the words. 'If this was anything more, you would stay for *you*—and for *us*; if you wanted there to be an "us". The fact I even have to tell you that says it all. You're not ready for this. Maybe you never will be. But I can't wait around for you to decide or watch while you make a half-hearted attempt at staying in one place when your heart isn't in it. What do you expect me to do? Give everything to someone I know one day will walk away? Why would anyone do that? Sometimes we have to be selfish to survive.'

It was more than she'd intended to say but she took consolation from the fact it was as close as she could get to the truth without telling him how she felt. Just to be on the safe side, she stepped back, rolling her lips together to stop anything else from slipping out.

'You done?'

'Yes.' She nodded. 'I'm done.'

When it looked as if he was going to reach for her, she took another step back. If he kissed her she wouldn't stand a chance. She shook her head. 'That won't solve anything.

It's not like we ever had a problem there. But if you care about me—even the tiniest little bit—you'll respect—'

'You think I *don't care*?' The question was thrown at her with enough force to rock her back on her heels. 'You think I *asked* for this? What gave you the impression I need additional complications in my life right now? I didn't ask for *any* of this.'

'You're not angry at me.'

'The *hell* I'm not.'

'Say it, just once.'

'Say *what*?'

'Who you're angry at.' Her voice cracked, the need to reach out, soothe and find the right thing to say to help him the way he'd helped her so intense it almost tore her apart. 'It's not me because who ended this doesn't matter. It was always going to end. So say it—don't stop to think about it—*who* are you angry at?'

'You want me to say my parents, don't you?' His lips slipped over his teeth in a movement closer to a sneer than a smile. 'You think you've got me all figured out. You want to know who I'm angry at, I'll tell you.' Taking a step closer, he allowed her to see the torment in the depths of his eyes. '*Me*. I'm. Angry. At. Myself. Happy now?'

How she felt couldn't have been further from happy but somehow, from somewhere, she found enough strength to continue looking into his eyes. 'Then maybe you should ask yourself why and find a way of fixing it, because even if you could stay in one place for long enough to work on a relationship, I couldn't fix that for you, not alone.'

Taking a step back, he turned his head and looked down the path they'd taken, a muscle clenching in his jaw before he swallowed hard and nodded, his voice hollow. 'I know.'

'But for the record—' she smiled tremulously when he glanced at her '—if you'd let me, I'd have tried.'

'I know.'

Prolonging the inevitable, she watched the blink of his thick lashes as he continued staring into the distance. But the longer she stood there and felt the invisible draw to him, the harder it would be to leave. Stepping closer, she placed a soft, lingering kiss on his cheek, taking a last breath of clean, masculine scent before saying the two most difficult words she'd ever had to say.

'Goodbye, Blake.'

CHAPTER THIRTEEN

'You're not ready for this.'

Thunder rolled ominously through heavy clouds pushing their way over the skyscrapers but Blake walked slowly, even when the heatwave broke; people ran for cover or rushed past him beneath plastic hooded tourist capes and assorted umbrellas.

'If this was anything more, you would stay for you—and for us; if you wanted there to be an "us".'

It was the light bulb moment it had taken for him to see things more clearly. As she'd said it he'd realised he wanted there to be an *'us'*. He wanted it so bad the thought of living without her felt as if he were being pulled apart on some kind of medieval torture rack. He wanted their lives so tangled up nothing could unravel the threads that bound them together. He wanted to hear her laughter and watch her sleep and be amused by the fact she never let a cup of coffee sit still long enough to cool on its own. He wanted to argue with her so they could make up. Have her push him to talk so he could understand things more clearly with a different point of view.

She had little patience, talked too much at times for his liking, hogged the hell out of the covers on their bed—which would have bugged him if they'd met in the winter—but she was smart and bright and funny and tenacious and braver than she realised. And it had taken her to leave for him to know he didn't want to let her go.

But he hadn't stopped her or gone after her because she was right—she couldn't fix him, not alone. Even if she could, he wouldn't let her. It was up to him to make sense of his life so he could offer her more than half a man. He just had to pray she wouldn't find a guy less messed up than him before he worked his way through it and could tell her the things he wanted to say.

The thought and accompanying surge of jealousy lent a sense of urgency to the situation. Stopping dead in his tracks, he ignored the rain falling heavily on his head and bouncing off the concrete around his feet while he gritted his teeth and attacked the emptiness head-on. He dug deep and searched for a place to begin. He refused to believe he couldn't heal himself and build a new life—one he could share with her.

He wasn't aware how long he stood there but it was not that difficult to find a starting point—not when the stakes were so high.

Reaching a hand to his pocket to check the envelope was there, he hailed a cab. Forty minutes later, it had stopped raining and he was walking purposefully along winding paths edged with majestic trees and immaculately tended lawns. It had been fourteen years since he'd been there, but he remembered the way. Beyond modest, moss-green lakes full of ducks and geese, past black squirrels scurrying from pines to lindens; he rounded the corner and pinpointed the weeping beech, its branches skirting the ground above the stones, one more weathered than the other.

Footsteps slowing, he looked around and decided it wasn't too bad a place to end up—peaceful, pretty and private. He was thankful for the latter considering what he was about to do. Reading the names on the stones, he felt the emptiness throb like an old injury he'd convinced himself he never had until he started to stretch the muscle again. He hadn't known Charlie had forgone the family mausoleum. It was nice. Good to know his mom wasn't alone any more. Just a pity they'd waited so long to get together.

'I'm not mad at you.' Their son took a deep breath and ignored the fact he felt like an idiot for talking out loud. 'Not any more. But I was, for a long time. You messed up. But I think you knew that. Least I hope you did. I want to forgive you for sucking as parents, but I can't throw stones in that department until I can prove I'm better at it than you. Maybe one day I'll be able to come back and tell you how I'm doing with that…'

Blake shook his head at how he had questioned his sudden need for a family. It wasn't sudden, but it wasn't just a family he wanted either. It was a family *with Liv*. That was why he couldn't let her go.

'I can't keep being angry or feeling frustrated but I won't blame you for that. I should have dealt with this earlier.' But instead he'd allowed parts of himself to wither away, without nurture, rather than risk getting involved with someone he might damage in the way his parents' actions had damaged him.

Trouble was, while he'd been so focused on the empty place inside him, he'd been ignoring the feelings that had been growing elsewhere.

When another wave of anger hit him that it had taken so long to figure it out he took several deep breaths and fought it off, shaking his head more firmly. He didn't have to make the same mistakes they had. Nor would he continue punishing himself for things that *hadn't* been his fault. He was who he was because of his upbringing but he didn't have to stay that way. He could break the cycle, be the man he chose to be and the kind of father he'd never had to his own kids. The kids he wanted to have some day with Liv, if she'd have him.

'This stops now. I'm sick of running in the wrong direction.' As his voice grew more determined, he felt stronger, the emptiness within him shrinking as if hope held it in a fist and was squeezing tighter with each word. 'There's a time to stand and fight for the things that matter. I've said it before but this time I mean it: I won't hide—not who I am, what I want or how I feel.'

Bet big to win big, that was how he saw it. But he wasn't carrying any IOUs from the past into his new life. Without hesitation, he reached for the envelope, pushed his thumb below the seal, ripped it open and took out the letter.

Leaning her wrists on the metal railing, Olivia tugged out her earplugs and bent forward, gasping for breath. She was *so* unfit. Lifting her head as she continued hauling in air, her gaze took in the Manhattan skyline, Brooklyn's waterfront and the Verrazano Narrows Bridge as the famous orange ferry approached the terminal nearby. She could smell the brine, feel the sea breeze against her damp skin and hear the slap of water against the pilings, but while the familiarity of home would ordinarily have offered a measure of comfort, no matter what she tried, nothing made her feel better. Not when he was gone.

At first it was the little things like the lack of messages on her phone or the sound of his voice when she called to see how his meetings had gone that reminded her of the loss, but since she'd been gradually weaning herself off those things she was able to cope with that. Waking up alone after a restless night of tossing and turning while she tried to find a comfortable sleeping position without his large body to curl into was harder. Seeing his face in several interviews hadn't helped. While she was incredibly proud he was taking on the press on his own terms, every time she found an article about Warren Enterprises' new owner, she absorbed it, reaching out and touching his face as if somehow the ink could transmit the warmth of his skin to her fingertips.

The last time she'd felt anything close to as empty as she did without him, it had taken a new career to get her through. She had put everything into it, filling her mind and the hours until one day merged into the next and she was able to take a breath without hurting. But no matter how hard she looked, she knew she would never find another man to replace Blake. What she was experiencing was self-inflicted grief. But if it hurt as much as this after ten days without him, she'd been right to let him go.

She had to continue believing that.

When another wave of emotion threatened to overwhelm her, she pushed off the railing and walked a circle as she put the earplugs back in and ramped up the volume. Picking up the pace, she pushed her body through the pain barrier, running harder to replace emotional pain with straining muscles, aching lungs and a raw throat. Couple more miles and she would return to the house she'd grown up in to shower and change, filling a few more Blakeless hours with a family barbecue for her niece's birthday, where she could smile and pretend everything was okay.

Even if it felt as if it never would be again.

'I'm pretty sure what you're doing to that chicken is illegal in five states,' Johnnie commented when they gathered around a picnic table in the park.

'And Canada...'

Olivia's gaze jerked sharply upward at the comment

from the second of her brothers as he clinked their beer bottles together. 'What was that?'

'What?' Danny asked.

'The Canada thing—what does it mean?'

'Can't tell you,' he replied with a completely straight face. 'We took an oath.'

She blinked. 'Who did you take an oath *with*?'

'Your boyfriend.' He shrugged.

'My what?'

'Your boyfriend.' Johnnie held his bottle up and spread his fingers. 'Clean record, lays on a pretty decent spread on poker night…'

'Are you talking about Blake?' When she lifted a trembling hand to swipe hair back from her face, she knocked over a plastic beaker, forcing her to scramble to catch it as her mother joined them.

'He sounded lovely on the phone this morning. I'm looking forward to meeting him.'

'You talked to him on the phone?'

Was there a hidden camera somewhere?

'When you went for your run,' her mom replied as if it was an everyday occurrence.

'Pretty straight-up guy,' Danny commented as he reached out a finger towards the icing on the birthday cake and had his hand slapped away. 'Dad would have liked him. He's good with his hands.'

Olivia felt a flush of warmth building on her neck. 'When did you meet Blake?'

'Last week,' Johnnie replied for Danny, looking across at his wife where she was talking to a couple of other mothers and watching Amy play with her friends. 'Wanted to check on the procedure for closing off a road down by a warehouse on the river, we got talking—he mentioned he played poker—so I invited him to the Monday night game.'

'He got dating approval when he lost the pot.' Danny smiled. 'Never mentioned you were dating a rich guy...'

Olivia frowned. 'How much money did you take off him?'

'Let's just say I don't need to worry about making the rent this month...'

Meaning Blake had lost on purpose. How had her brothers not known that? If they were tag-teaming him she was going to kick their—

'He'll tell you about it when he gets here.'

'When he gets here?' On a day when she had virtually no make-up on, still had puffy eyes and—

'Yeah, we figured you were making things difficult for him.' Danny nodded. 'We told him to hang in there.'

'Speak of the devil.' Johnnie smiled.

'Oh, my,' her mother said. 'Isn't he handsome?'

He was also a dead man. Did he think she'd endured ten days of hell so she could go through it all over again? Olivia closed her eyes and took a deep breath before facing him, knowing full well the very sight of him would do what it had done from the get-go. When she turned around her heart crumpled into a tight, painful ball in her chest.

Damn it. It was *so* unfair he looked that good.

She hated him for it.

Blake smiled as Liv headed straight for him with a glint in her eyes that said he was in trouble.

She was beautiful when she was mad.

'What are you doing here?' she bit out, grabbing hold of his sleeve and turning him around without breaking stride.

'I was invited. Didn't the guys mention it?'

'Oh, believe me, they're next on my list.' She cocked an accusatory brow at him. 'And you called my *mother*?'

'What do I know about buying a present for a three-year-old girl?' He held up the bag in his hand. 'I've never bought anything this pink in my life.'

'What are you even doing buying a gift for my niece? We broke up, remember?' She frowned, glancing over her shoulder before she dragged him behind a tree. Letting go of his sleeve, she took a step back. 'Why are you here?'

'Why do you think I'm here?'

'Would I ask if I knew?'

'Have a think about it for a minute.'

When she floundered, he smiled, unable to resist when it had been the longest ten days he'd ever experienced. Lifting his hand, he slid his fingers around the nape of her neck and lowered his head, not caring who might be watching as he fitted his mouth to hers. It felt like a lifetime since he'd kissed her and Blake knew, without a shadow of doubt, he would never, *ever* get enough of her.

He just had to convince her to give them a chance.

When he looked down at her, she still had her eyes closed, her lower lip trembling as she took a long, ragged breath. Her lashes lifted, her gaze meeting his with a flash of vulnerability that completely did him in.

She shook her head, her voice thick. 'I can't do this again.'

'You won't have to.'

Any doubts he'd had disappeared as her eyes filled with tears. While she was crumbling in front of him and his chest cramped, relief washed over him. They weren't so different. She'd been struggling to deal with what was happening between them as much as he had.

'Thought I wouldn't figure out what you were doing?' Before she could say anything, he took her hand and led her to a bench below the tree. 'Sit.'

'I don't want to sit.' She tugged on her hand and sniffed loudly. 'I want you to go away.'

'Do I have to kiss you again?'

'Blake, you can't—'

'Yes, I can.' Tightening his fingers around hers, he pinned her in place with a determined gaze, silently transmitting all of the frustration and longing he'd experienced without her as he fought an internal battle with his need to demonstrate—the old-fashioned way—just how much he wanted her.

Her eyes widened.

'Sit,' he said roughly.

'No.' She frowned.

'Fine, then we'll do this standing up.' Unwilling to release her hand in case she made an attempt at leaving him again, he set the bag at his feet and took a steadying breath. 'Thought I was the one who ran away.'

'I—'

'Got scared.' He lifted his brows. 'You think I don't know how that feels?'

Her swollen lips formed words that never came. A frown, a short breath and then she blinked. 'I didn't think…I mean I thought…'

'No.' He shook his head, the sight of the strong-willed woman who had him wrapped around her little finger struggling to form a sentence creating an overwhelming swell of emotion inside him. 'You didn't. But I didn't help any with that, did I?'

'We knew this wouldn't last,' she protested weakly.

'Did we?' he asked again as he looked deep into her eyes. It might have been true at the start, but things had changed. At least they had for him.

'You don't stay in one place for long.'

'I never stayed in one place for long because I've never

known anything else.' That part she knew, so he tried to explain the cycle the way he understood it with the perspective he'd gained, thanks to her. 'Because I kept moving, I never got attached to anyone. Because I never got attached to anyone, there was nothing to stop me leaving. I didn't think I needed a place to call home. But for a place to be a home I think it needs to be more than just a place. And since I'd never got attached to anyone…'

'There was no one to come home to…'

He smiled. 'Not till now.'

When her brows wavered, he reached out and tucked a strand of hair behind her ear, his fingers lingering on the sensitive skin on her neck before he lowered his arm. Taking another deep breath, he started to lay his cards on the table the way he'd rehearsed over and over again.

'You were right,' he told her. 'I needed to figure out why I was angry and do something to fix it. It wasn't something you could do for me. I wouldn't have let you try. I'm not saying I'm all the way there but I made a start. Thing is, what you said about not being able to do it alone? That's how I feel, Liv. I don't want to do it alone. I feel better when you're there. You're the first person I've ever wanted to run to.'

When her lips parted on a low gasp, he took a half step forward. 'I know I don't make it easy, that's why I need someone in my life who will tell me when I'm being a jerk and kick me into touch when I need it; someone who knows to push to get me to talk things through, even when I don't want to. I need you, Liv. You've no idea how much I need you. You're it for me in ways I can't even begin to explain but I tried to show you when I couldn't find words.'

'I didn't know that's what you were doing,' she said in an impossibly soft voice.

A corner of his mouth tugged wryly. 'Neither did I at the time, but I get it now. It makes sense.'

'It does.' She nodded, but her smile was tentative, as if she still couldn't quite believe what she was hearing.

'I thought about what I wanted.' He threaded his fingers more firmly through hers. 'And I'm here to tell you. I'm ready for this. Now I need to know if you are.'

'I'm terrified,' she confessed.

'Know what scares me?'

She shook her head.

'Losing you.' When her eyes shimmered again he choked, 'Please don't do that, sweetheart.'

'You just gotta give me a minute.'

He held his breath and counted to ten as she blinked and took several deep breaths, reminding him of the time he'd felt her shaking and had held her until it had stopped. While they were the same in many ways, he realised when they'd met they had been at the opposite ends of the scale. Where he'd been struggling to feel things, she'd kept her emotions tightly in check because she felt things so strongly.

'Is that long enough?'

There was a short burst of laughter and then her brows lifted, her voice filled with incredulity as she asked, 'You thought infiltrating my family was the best way to come tell me all this?'

'I couldn't come tell you till I'd fixed as much as I could on my own,' he explained. 'I had to sort out my life so I had one to share with you. I'd planned to come find you when I'd worked through it, but when Johnnie landed at the warehouse and invited me to poker night—lame as it sounds—spending time with your brothers made me feel closer to you till I could see you again. They're like you, you know. You're better-looking, obviously, but they have the same sense of humour and say similar things and they're as proud of how you rebuilt your life after being a cop as I am—not that I had anything to do with it. You know they still worry about you, right?'

'They worry too much.'

'Yeah, I got that. I told them you can take care of yourself.' He didn't tell her the grilling that had accompanied his defence of her when there were still more important things to say. Didn't matter, anyway—he could handle her brothers. 'Talking about you helped. I missed you but I wasn't going to come to you damaged. You deserve better than that.'

'We're all damaged,' she said in a firmer voice as she squeezed his fingers. 'Why do you think this scares me so much? I tried not to care, really I did, but I couldn't stop it happening and when I knew how I felt—knowing you would leave—'

'I'm not going anywhere. I didn't stop to think about how long I'd been in New York this time till Marty opened his trap and pointed it out, but I'd already been here longer than I've ever stayed in one place.' The corner of his mouth tugged wryly. 'I told myself it was because we were busy but the truth is I've been coming back here for years—even if I never found an apartment to stay in. When I left it was more about going where the work was than running away from anything but, now I've thought about it, I think it was a sign I was ready to stay in one place and put down some roots.'

'If you'd told me that I would never have left.'

'If you hadn't left it might have taken me longer to work my way through everything. The thought of losing you proved quite the motivator.' Even thinking about it when she was in front of him created a wave of desperation. He needed everything out in the open, for it to be crystal clear so there was no room for doubt.

Clearing his throat a little less silently than he'd have preferred, he flexed his fingers around hers. 'If we do this, Liv, I need to warn you there'll be no leaving me again. Wherever you go, I'll find you and bring you home so we can work our way through the tough stuff together. I'm talking the whole package here. We'll start slow this time if that's what you need to believe what I'm telling you, but I want to marry you, have kids with you and spend the rest of our lives—'

'Yes.'

Suddenly finding it difficult to breathe, he shook his head. 'You might want to think it through before you give me an answer. I swear I'll be the best husband to you I possibly can but I'm not always gonna get it right. I'm far from perfect. I like to think I'm getting better at the whole talking things through thing but there'll still be times I'll struggle with that. Old habits...'

'You're doing fine.' She smiled.

'We'll still argue.'

'I know.' She shrugged a shoulder. 'But fighting with you kinda turns me on a little bit.'

'It does, does it?'

She nodded. 'Uh-huh.'

'Me, too.' He smiled in reply.

Liv took a small step forward, their bodies inches apart. 'We have a pretty great time making up.'

'Yes, we do.' He looked deep into her eyes. 'But it won't always be the solution to everything. We'll both have to work at this.'

'We will,' she agreed.

'But so long as you're happy, I'm happy, and if there's

anything within my power to give you than you'll damn well *let me* give you—'

'Never thought I'd say this, but could you stop talking for a minute?' She smiled the smile he hadn't wanted to understand until he was searching for something he desperately needed to be there. 'The answer is still yes. I don't need to think about it and I don't need to take it slow. Now we've fixed the communication problem I think we can get through anything together. Neither of us is perfect. Thing is, I don't want perfect. Just as well really, considering I'm in love with you and you can be a giant pain in the—'

'You have no idea how much I missed you,' he said hoarsely, what he could see in her eyes and hear in her voice banishing the last of the emptiness within him and filling it with warmth and light and more love than he had ever thought he could feel for another human being.

'I do if it's half as much as I missed you.' Tears shimmered in her eyes again as she laid a hand on his chest, directly over his thundering heart. 'I was miserable without you.'

Framing her face with his hand, he caught a tear with the tip of his thumb as it spilled from the corner of her eye. 'Me, too. In case you hadn't got it already, I love you, Liv. I've never loved anyone the way I love you. I never will. You're it for me. No more hiding, no more secrets from here on in— What's wrong?'

He frowned as she leaned back and grimaced.

'I found the letter from your father. When we were packing, it fell out of your pocket.'

Wait. 'Was that what happened? There was something about the letter that bothered you?'

'No—' she shook her head '—I wanted to ask you about it, but I couldn't. Every time you shared something with me and I felt closer to you, there was more to lose. I thought

I could distance myself and shut off my emotions, but it was too late. I'm strong, Blake, but…'

'I know you are.'

'Not all the time. I thought letting you go would be easier than watching you leave, but it wasn't.'

'Come here.'

When she stepped in to him and wrapped her arms around his waist, he held her close and frowned at the shudder running through her body. 'You're shaking.'

'Emotional overload,' she said against his chest. 'I might have held it all inside for too long.'

'You don't have to hold anything back from me.'

'Because you looked so happy when I got weepy?'

'Cry, laugh out loud, yell your head off if you need to let something out—I want it all, Liv.'

'Remember you said that the next time I yell at you.' He heard her smile. 'Now tell me about the letter.'

Blake laid his cheek against her hair. 'I carried it too long. Wasn't ready to read it or didn't want to face what was in it when I heard he was gone; doesn't really matter now. I carried a lot of things around for too long. I read it. A lot of it I expected, some of it I didn't. He mentioned the will—you can look at it if you like.'

'No. It's the last letter from a father to his son.'

'Explains a lot about my relationship with him I'd like you to know. I want you to know everything in the same way I want to know everything about you.'

'We have time.' She smiled as she leaned back and her gaze met his. Her feelings glowed in her eyes as she pressed an all too brief kiss to his mouth. 'I love you.'

'I love you, too.' He smiled back and leaned in for a more meaningful kiss; the kind that reminded him how long it had been since they'd shared a bed and made him want to get to one so he could demonstrate more eloquently how he felt when three small words didn't feel like enough.

She sighed when he lifted his head. 'You better come meet the rest of the family before they send out a search party and find us making out.'

'We'll tell them we just got engaged.' He thought about the ring he'd been carrying around in his pocket for more than a week—the past replaced by his hope for the future. It was tempting to give it to her since she'd already said yes and she didn't have a hope in hell of ever taking it back, but he had plans for when he put that ring on her finger. Ones that didn't involve a public place or an audience...

She laughed softly. 'This soon? No, we won't. They'll think I'm pregnant.'

'I'm willing to work on that.' He grinned. 'And since you're using up all the vacation time you've saved over the last few years instead of working on one of those big litigation cases you talked about when you dumped me...'

'Oh, my God—' she rolled her eyes as she leaned back '—is there anything my brothers didn't tell you?'

'Not much after I'd dropped a couple of hands.'

'Don't do that again,' she warned as he reached for the birthday present he'd left at her feet. 'They won't respect you for it.'

'I'll keep that in mind when they come to our place for poker night.' He kept hold of her hand as they walked around the tree.

'You're going to tell me about Canada now, right?'

'When we're married and you can't testify against me.'

'Blake.'

'Yes?'

'Blake.'

He stopped and turned towards her, allowing the meaning to seep into his soul as he heard *'I want you'* wrapped in *'I love you'* and knew with a certainty he hoped all men felt when the time came to settle and put down roots, he'd found his place in the world. Wherever she was would be home for the rest of his life.

'I hear you,' he said roughly. She'd spoken to him from the start, even when she wasn't using words. 'And for the record, I'm your man, Liv. I always will be.'

All it had taken was for her to come find him when he hadn't known he was looking.

* * * * *

ROMANCE

Jewel in His Crown	Lynne Graham
The Man Every Woman Wants	Miranda Lee
Once a Ferrara Wife...	Sarah Morgan
Not Fit for a King?	Jane Porter
In Bed with a Stranger	India Grey
In a Storm of Scandal	Kim Lawrence
The Call of the Desert	Abby Green
Playing His Dangerous Game	Tina Duncan
How to Win the Dating War	Aimee Carson
Interview with the Daredevil	Nicola Marsh
Snowbound with Her Hero	Rebecca Winters
The Playboy's Gift	Teresa Carpenter
The Tycoon Who Healed Her Heart	Melissa James
Firefighter Under the Mistletoe	Melissa McClone
Flirting with Italian	Liz Fielding
The Inconvenient Laws of Attraction	Trish Wylie
The Night Before Christmas	Alison Roberts
Once a Good Girl...	Wendy S. Marcus

HISTORICAL

The Disappearing Duchess	Anne Herries
Improper Miss Darling	Gail Whitiker
Beauty and the Scarred Hero	Emily May
Butterfly Swords	Jeannie Lin

MEDICAL ROMANCE™

New Doc in Town	Meredith Webber
Orphan Under the Christmas Tree	Meredith Webber
Surgeon in a Wedding Dress	Sue MacKay
The Boy Who Made Them Love Again	Scarlet Wilson

ROMANCE

Bride for Real	Lynne Graham
From Dirt to Diamonds	Julia James
The Thorn in His Side	Kim Lawrence
Fiancée for One Night	Trish Morey
Australia's Maverick Millionaire	Margaret Way
Rescued by the Brooding Tycoon	Lucy Gordon
Swept Off Her Stilettos	Fiona Harper
Mr Right There All Along	Jackie Braun

HISTORICAL

Ravished by the Rake	Louise Allen
The Rake of Hollowhurst Castle	Elizabeth Beacon
Bought for the Harem	Anne Herries
Slave Princess	Juliet Landon

MEDICAL ROMANCE™

Flirting with the Society Doctor	Janice Lynn
When One Night Isn't Enough	Wendy S. Marcus
Melting the Argentine Doctor's Heart	Meredith Webber
Small Town Marriage Miracle	Jennifer Taylor
St Piran's: Prince on the Children's Ward	Sarah Morgan
Harry St Clair: Rogue or Doctor?	Fiona McArthur

1111 GEN STD LP

Mills & Boon® Hardback

January 2012

ROMANCE

The Man Who Risked It All	Michelle Reid
The Sheikh's Undoing	Sharon Kendrick
The End of her Innocence	Sara Craven
The Talk of Hollywood	Carole Mortimer
Secrets of Castillo del Arco	Trish Morey
Hajar's Hidden Legacy	Maisey Yates
Untouched by His Diamonds	Lucy Ellis
The Secret Sinclair	Cathy Williams
First Time Lucky?	Natalie Anderson
Say It With Diamonds	Lucy King
Master of the Outback	Margaret Way
The Reluctant Princess	Raye Morgan
Daring to Date the Boss	Barbara Wallace
Their Miracle Twins	Nikki Logan
Runaway Bride	Barbara Hannay
We'll Always Have Paris	Jessica Hart
Heart Surgeon, Hero...Husband?	Susan Carlisle
Doctor's Guide to Dating in the Jungle	Tina Beckett

HISTORICAL

The Mysterious Lord Marlowe	Anne Herries
Marrying the Royal Marine	Carla Kelly
A Most Unladylike Adventure	Elizabeth Beacon
Seduced by Her Highland Warrior	Michelle Willingham

MEDICAL

The Boss She Can't Resist	Lucy Clark
Dr Langley: Protector or Playboy?	Joanna Neil
Daredevil and Dr Kate	Leah Martyn
Spring Proposal in Swallowbrook	Abigail Gordon

ROMANCE

The Kanellis Scandal	Michelle Reid
Monarch of the Sands	Sharon Kendrick
One Night in the Orient	Robyn Donald
His Poor Little Rich Girl	Melanie Milburne
From Daredevil to Devoted Daddy	Barbara McMahon
Little Cowgirl Needs a Mum	Patricia Thayer
To Wed a Rancher	Myrna Mackenzie
The Secret Princess	Jessica Hart

HISTORICAL

Seduced by the Scoundrel	Louise Allen
Unmasking the Duke's Mistress	Margaret McPhee
To Catch a Husband...	Sarah Mallory
The Highlander's Redemption	Marguerite Kaye

MEDICAL

The Playboy of Harley Street	Anne Fraser
Doctor on the Red Carpet	Anne Fraser
Just One Last Night...	Amy Andrews
Suddenly Single Sophie	Leonie Knight
The Doctor & the Runaway Heiress	Marion Lennox
The Surgeon She Never Forgot	Melanie Milburne

1211 GEN STD LP